GRIM TALES

SURREY & SUSSEX

Edited by Donna Samworth

First published in Great Britain in 2015 by:

 Young**Writers**

Remus House
Coltsfoot Drive
Peterborough
PE2 9BF
Telephone: 01733 890066
Website: www.youngwriters.co.uk
Book Design by Tim Christian & Ashley Janson
SB ISBN 978-1-78443-754-1

Printed and bound in the UK by BookPrintingUK
Website: www.bookprintinguk.com

FOREWORD

Welcome, Reader!

For Young Writers' latest competition, Grim Tales, we gave secondary school pupils nationwide the tricky task of writing a story with a beginning, middle and an end in just 100 words. They could either write a completely original tale or add a twist to a well-loved classic. They rose to the challenge magnificently!

We chose stories for publication based on style, expression, imagination and technical skill. The result is this entertaining collection full of diverse and imaginative mini sagas, which is also a delightful keepsake to look back on in years to come.

Here at Young Writers our aim is to encourage creativity in young adults and to inspire a love of the written word, so it's great to get such an amazing response, with some absolutely fantastic stories. This made it a tough challenge to pick the winners, so well done to Annabell Agate who has been chosen as the best author in this anthology.

I'd like to congratulate all the young authors in Grim Tales - Surrey & Sussex - I hope this inspires them to continue with their creative writing. And who knows, maybe we'll be seeing their names on the best seller lists in the future...

Jenni Bannister

Editorial Manager

CONTENTS

FARLINGTON SCHOOL, HORSHAM

GREENFIELDS SCHOOL, FOREST ROW

GREENSHAW HIGH SCHOOL, SUTTON

HURSTPIERPOINT COLLEGE SENIOR, HASSOCKS

LIMPSFIELD GRANGE SCHOOL, OXTED

OASIS ACADEMY SHIRLEY PARK, CROYDON

OLD PALACE OF JOHN WHITGIFT SCHOOL, CROYDON

ORIEL HIGH SCHOOL, CRAWLEY

REED'S SCHOOL, COBHAM

REIGATE GRAMMAR SCHOOL, REIGATE

STEYNING GRAMMAR SCHOOL, STEYNING

THE
MINI SAGAS

Two Wolves...

A long time ago, in a cold place, a man sat near a fire with a wrinkled old face. His grandson sat close, leaning in for the tale. The man tapped his nose and said with a grin, 'The story is horror, and it shall begin. Deep down inside you, a battle does rage, two wolves, just two, one is good, the other is bad, loved, and hated, misunderstood.' The boy was confused so he said, 'But which one is bruised?' The man smiled with a glint in his eye, 'Why my dear child, It's the wolf you feed... '

ISOBEL GALE (13)

Snow White

'You buffoon,' shrieked the dark queen throwing the cow's heart against the wall.
'I wanted Snow White's.' She turned, smiling slyly, 'But for now you will do!' she cackled and plunged a dagger into the huntsman, removing his heart. The queen took things into her own hands. She poisoned an apple and, dressing as a hag, she went to the home of Snow White. Snow ate the apple and fell into a deep sleep. She was placed in a glass coffin outside the house, the prince arrived and kissed Snow but... she never woke up!

ELLIE RABY (13)

1

HUNTING SNOW WHITE IN NEW YORK

He ran, chasing the girl into the forest of concrete buildings. Sirens of cars pierced the ears. Tiny screams, as the girl's yellow dress was painted brown with muddy water. He would catch her. He would never betray the queen. He never did.

Knife and rope in hand, he headed for the bridge, stopping to look in the Pound Store. Tantalising visions of ice cream makers he could enjoy. Suddenly, a whirlwind from above, clanking of metal, clicks of guns and a loud noise as a shadow dropped behind him.

'The name's Bond, James Bond.'

Bang! Snow White was safe.

HANNAH SNELLING (12)

THE LIFE OF AN ARTIST

I sat on the small wooden bench, notebook in one hand and pencil in the other. All around me there were couples and families, children, pets and picnic baskets. Laughter and singing filled the air. The more of life that exploded around me, the faster I drew, eager to catch all of life's mysteries on one simple, innocent page.

This is the life of an artist. A life of observance, of watching colours unfurl around me. You could call me a mirror I suppose. But for me, sharing tales is the only true way not to lose them forever.

EMMA FOX (16)

THE GIRL AND THE WINDOW

'That'll teach you!' spat her ferocious father, slamming the door; the twist of a key left her trapped. She clutched her cheek as a rivulet of blood, tears and mascara trickled to the floor.
Climbing onto the window ledge, her hair rippled like silk behind her, as a cool breeze soothed her stinging pain. The moon seemed to beckon with its comforting glow... Her eyes darted round the room, landing on candles as they flickered innocently. With a nudge of her foot, furious flames of vengeance danced across the room. She took off into the sky. Freedom was hers.

ELLIE HETHERINGTON BOSTOCK-SMITH (12)

ACCOMPANIED LONELINESS

The trees began to sway. The whistling of the brisk wind overshadowed many thoughts of the explorer. His steps were carefully quick through a pathway that wound through the forest. The descending sun drained the vibrant, charismatic colours of the sapling. Deafening silence began to fill the quickly awakening atmosphere. Suddenly, sounds became ever present. As if several shrubs were whispering amongst themselves, recounting long-lived memories they once shared. Quietly then louder, louder! Just then, he knew. Dread, fear, loneliness engulfed his ever-growing mindful thoughts. He finally realised he wasn't the only one in the vast, scary woodland.

ALEXANDER LUCAS ELDAIEF (14)
ACS Egham International School, Egham

The Loud Creature

Boom! Boom! Boom! The sound of rushing footsteps came through the hallway. My mother shouted something. Still in shock, I packed all my things. I rushed into my sister's room and woke her up. We didn't have much time. The loud bangs were getting louder and closer, coming from downstairs. *Boom! Boom!* I was scared. I decided to look outside. My dad's car was parked near the door and I wondered where he was. My sister screamed at the sound of a loud thump. It was my dad knocking, trying to open the door. He'd left his keys inside.

Alim Aubakirov (14)
ACS Egham International School, Egham

Big Blue Eyes

My sister's like me. Big blue eyes, smattering of freckles, wild hair. Missing posters line the lamp posts. A boy, my friend since I could smile, his face smack on the front. Salty tears line my eyelashes, missing, the boy who went missing.
Everyone's asleep, I climb up to my freckled sister's room. Silence. Where is she? I check her bed, bathroom, closet. And there, the boy who went missing, straining against duct tape and rope. A figure hunched over him, I stagger back. There, looking at me through twisted locks, are big blue eyes and a smattering of freckles.

Linnea Emanuelson (15)
ACS Egham International School, Egham

I Am A God!

Everything slipped away. Lifeless. Just blue and yellow. Not really feeling my crackling skin. Pure exhaustion. Metallic taste and smell of dust. A camel! The surge of hope gave me chills. I would live! Conscious again, I hoisted myself onto the camel. Three policeman came around the corner of a pyramid. The camel ran. The wind picked up and sand-papered my skin. The ground began to collapse. It all happened so fast. I slipped away.
When I awoke, pharaohs bowed down to me. I was sitting on a throne with a cat beside me. They thought I was a god!

CAOIMHE STEWART (15)
ACS Egham International School, Egham

Hung Shame

Eyes fell upon my head wrapped in shame, sweat danced across my forehead. The rope got tighter as my fingers numbed. I could feel the audience's hate strangle my tortured soul. I felt jaded as the man spoke of my sins. I stood on my tiptoes as I was having a staring contest with Death, in a matter of inches I would blink. I searched the crowd for a loved one, for a memory to calm my racing heart. The noose tightened and my eyes started to slowly shut, blinded by the afternoon sun. I realised a thief dies alone.

NICHOLAS MARSAGLIA
ACS Egham International School, Egham

ONE PIZZA COULD SAVE YOUR LIFE

The little boy's parents left for dinner but forgot to give him and his sister money for pizza. He turned on the living room's black box. 'Nothing!' he said. Then came across an 18-rated movie. He got seizures from his hunger. He was now passed out and lying on the floor when the electricity went out. He hovered back on his feet, his sister was angry and came to blame it on him. After that all I can say is that the little boy wasn't hungry anymore when his parents came back he had an appetite for them too.

DARYLL CASPAR NETSCHER (15)
ACS Egham International School, Egham

THE PREDATOR'S WORLD

He appeared on the tarpaulin. Quivering with fear, he watched my antics suspiciously. His astonishment at my appearance was gradually replaced by rage and fear. His friend was different; in body and mind. She appeared melancholy after climbing aboard; gazing at the distant horizon. A scent was in the air. This was prey. The sweet aroma made me salivate. I attacked the source and devoured it over several days. A cry ran through the air. She was agitated. We faced each other and howled. She was now a threat. Crazed with hunger, I decapitated her. And then, the alpha appeared...

ABHISHEK CHATTERJEE (14)
ACS Egham International School, Egham

TOO LATE

He fell to the ground, just like the apple. He watched from a distance, frozen, powerless. Her skin as white as snow. Breathless he wanted to scream, cry, fight. But all that came out was a whisper. 'Stay.' How could he not have saved her, when all he ever wanted was her love? He used all of his strength to pull himself up, but he still felt numb. Heartbroken. He walked up the stairs, picking up her shoe on his way up. Her hair was as long and beautiful as ever. He gave her one last kiss. One first breath.

FLOORTJE HOSMAN (15)
ACS Egham International School, Egham

HOCKEY

The crackling of the ice strikes beneath us. The time is now. We skate and skate until the legs of our bodies disappear. Millions are watching. The last few minutes are upcoming. It's 2-2. Overtime! One more push and I could be to that puck. Me! I can be the one to score that winning goal! I give it my all, I skate my hardest, when I realise, suddenly, my legs give away. I've lost the feeling in my legs from skating too hard. The doctor says I'll never play again. I love the game and always will. Go team.

TYLER COOPER (14)
ACS Egham International School, Egham

GREATEST FEAR

I was alone again, it all seemed like a routine to me now; the loneliness, the abandonment. Roaming down the cobbled streets of this messed-up village, the things that had occurred would always stick with me. It is intriguing how much pain can change someone. I was being followed by a little girl. It might have just been a crazy coincidence. But after twenty everlasting minutes of this game of tag that never ended, I turned and looked straight at her. She was brunette with great brown eyes. We stared at each other. I was shocked. She was me.

ANTONIA MEIER (14)
ACS Egham International School, Egham

THE SCARING CROW

A child lays dead in the alley. A hole in her chest. The smell of powder lingers in the air. A man standing over her, holding a smoking gun. He turns and leaves. Stepping over the body, he smiles. His bullet had found its mark.
Police arrive later that night. The man watches the body being taken. He sighs, knowing this is a one-man battle. If he speaks, he will be thrown into the asylum.
In a barn, a raven caws in pain. Its wing shot. A deep caw of revenge. Beak dripping crimson red from a murdered child.

HENRY LINTON (15)
ACS Egham International School, Egham

The Sniper

He took his aim. He turned off the safety. He squeezed the trigger. The shot fired. The gun's stock smashed hard into his shoulder. The sound was heard. The muzzle flash was seen. The cartridge sank into the soft desert floor. The bullet flew. The bullet span faster and faster until the bullet smashed into its target and drew blood. The target tried to fire back but couldn't because of the hole in his chest. He tried to call for help but it was too late. The target died and the sniper loaded another round, to kill again.

Alex Maier (12)
ACS Egham International School, Egham

Little Red Riding Wolf

He haunted me. Since my parents died. Since I started to live with my grandma. Since the woodchopper killed him. The wolf. Night and day his spirit would follow me. The noise of his howl would be hanging in my ear, keeping me awake at night. My dreams became nightmares. My life became a horror. I screamed in a corner, shaking and afraid. I couldn't keep this in anymore. I returned to the woods, somewhere his spirit would never find me. I ran away, hoping never to come back; but I left one thing, my precious Little Red Riding Hood.

Camila Meier (13)
ACS Egham International School, Egham

Two Opposites

There is a world split in half. One half is filled with nature, and the other half is a desert. There are tribes on both sides of the world and they often fight whenever they would meet at the border tree. So a rule was set out that no one was to go near the border and no one was allowed to cross it. Only two people ever broke that rule, they were both from opposite sides of the tree. Curiosity drew them to the tree. When they met, they shared their knowledge and brought it back to their tribes.

Annika Fernandez (12)
ACS Egham International School, Egham

The Mysterious Thief

Tyrone heard a noise behind him. He turned around, but it was too late. The man who was now running away had stolen his bag of money. It was the first time he had been robbed since his parents died. Searching for the thief, Tyrone found a cave. Inside there was a man tied up. It was the thief. Tyrone was a good person and untied him. The thief said, 'You have proven you are a generous person and for that I will give you this chest full of gold.' The thief disappeared and left a wooden chest for Tyrone.

Pablo Fernández-Trabadelo (12)
ACS Egham International School, Egham

THE THREE LITTLE PIGS

Once there were three little pigs. They were the sisters of *those* three little pigs. They grew up, always in the shadow of their brothers, but instead of fooling around, acting like the class clowns, barely making Cs but being able to go play football anyway like them, they worked hard in school and they each got scholarships to prestigious colleges like Harvard, Penn and Johns Hopkins. They became accomplished doctors, lawyers and scientists. They won Nobel prizes, impossible court battles, and discovered the cure for the common cold. Now those three little pigs live in their basements, futures untold.

ANGELA BARDEN (12)
ACS Egham International School, Egham

A GRIM STORY

She knew she was being followed as she walked through the woods. A tree branch cracked behind her. She looked around for any sign of the animal but she saw nothing. She heard a growl. The wolf then emerged from the shadows. Immediately she knew what it was, this was the wolf from all the fairy tales that her parents told to scare her when she was a child.
She started running. She knew that the wolf would not leave the woods and was gaining on her, but, as he was about to get her, she reached her grandma's house!

ELOI DE CLERCQ (15)
ACS Egham International School, Egham

The Not-So-Happy End

'Snow White!' she called menacingly.
Fear drove me away into the gloomy forest. She wanted me killed at noon. Tears, blood and sweat trickled down my face as I stumbled into a clearing to a welcoming house. Too tired to care, I entered and made myself at home.
Hours later I woke up to seven curious faces staring down at me. Dwarfs.
Time passed and I settled in, although one day an old crooked lady gave me an apple which brought me to my knees. It was her. The queen. Unconscious for days, but my perfect Prince Charming never came!

MIA GERRMANN (13)
ACS Egham International School, Egham

Little Red

Sweat dripped off my face, I was running to Grandma's. I tripped over a branch and everything fell out of my basket. Before I stood up I heard a crunch. I looked around and saw nothing. A low growl came from my left. I ran, I reached Grandma's, something was different.
'What big ears you have.'
'The better to hear you with.'
'What big eyes you have.'
'The better to see you with.'
'But what big teeth you have!'
Grandma grinned. 'The better to eat you with.'
I was swallowed by darkness and my red cloak drifted to the floor.

CLARE BOWDEN (12)
ACS Egham International School, Egham

The Leather

He pulled back the string of his bow, ready to fire an arrow at his prey. It was standing in the shore. He could not vacillate now. He fired the arrow but it did not catch its target. It had been swallowed by something. He fired at the water where it had been standing a moment before. His arrows hit nothing. He ran to where his prey had been standing. Nothing. Just the water. His feet were trapped by some leathery thing. He fell into the water. He was dragged to the depths. He looked down. Leather. Darkness swallowed him.

Mercedes Pascual (12)
ACS Egham International School, Egham

Little Red Riding Hood

The sound of footsteps thudding behind me as I walked across the forest, step by step. The smell of the cookies enriched the air. Top leaves rustled behind my path; there it stood, the wolf. Panic tickled through my spine, I sprinted to Grandmother's house. There it stood; a little cottage right before my eyes with Grandma awaiting my arrival. I jolted through the door, yet the wolf followed. Grandma blurted out a scream but the wolf pursued his target, with a large grunt he spread his mouth, engulfing Grandma as a whole. I stood there in shock. Goodbye Grandma.

Sonia Ali (14)
ACS Egham International School, Egham

THE MAN IN THE BLACK COAT

The town always speaks of that one man. The man who has blood as cold as ice, and a smile that evokes fear. He wears a black coat and never takes it off. Jimmy Burns says he's seen what's under the coat. Jimmy says, 'It was the body of a child. I saw it all, a mangled figure it was.'
Suddenly, he approaches me. I feel scared. My arm begins to shake. My skin becomes pale. He reaches inside his cloak, is this the end? What he gives me, is a piece of candy. He smiles and so do I.

ARDHIKA WIKRAMADARYANA (14)
ACS Egham International School, Egham

PLEASURE TO CRAZINESS

Patricia was the most 'uncool' girl in school, but she'd had enough. She bought a magic lamp but, little did she know, the lamp had an unknown side effect. She wished for all the cool kids to be uncool like her forever, but the side affect happened and all the cool people in the world turned ugly. Her face was all over the news with quotes: 'I've turned into the most ugly girl in the world'. Her own pleasure had turned into her end and slowly she turned crazy. She now lives in an asylum and hasn't been seen since.

KYLE PETTIGREW (14)
ACS Egham International School, Egham

BLUEBEARD

The woman opened the door and was hit by the stench of rotting flesh and long dried blood. There, on the walls were dead bodies. Bodies of women, his previous wives. The girl went nauseous. That is what he did to those who looked into the chamber. He killed them and pinned them to the wall like butterflies. She shut the door, turned around and was met by the pair of bright blue eyes. 'You looked into the chamber! The same fate awaits you!' He raised his long knife, and an arrow pierced his throat. The bowman was her brother.

DANIYAR KRYUKOV (13)
ACS Egham International School, Egham

SHE JUST DOESN'T SEE IT

This girl is so oblivious. Divided by two groups; one is kind, sweet and appreciative, the others thuggish, standoffish and rude, but most of all popular. All girls these days just choose popularity and attention, so with the wrong group chosen she goes about her life oblivious to the better choices she had. With all that said, I just rest my head, tired of my attempted persuasions, she made her choice, simply refusing to hear the sound of my voice I just stand back watching them hit that acting whack and talking oblivious to it. Blind to it.

JAKE MACKINTOSH (15)
ACS Egham International School, Egham

Broken

Smoke clings to the seams of her worn-out hoodie, it rises to the roof, the dim light-bulb of the room always comes back in. Her lips are dry, mouth thick from so many bites, fingers tremble as she lifts the lighter. Black nails, black circles under her eyes, black holes where her heart used to be. Her cheeks are wet with tears, ears aching from the roar of the music. He walks into the smoke-blinded room and just for a moment, the pieces of her broken heart are finally put back together again.

Cassi Neigh (15)
ACS Egham International School, Egham

The Chozzyfying Illusionistic Lady

The sweets were really delightful. So was the lady. But what I and Maya didn't anticipate was the illusion, she put forward to us. An illusion, so deadly. A truth so unexpected. And now, as we rush through this deep, unfathomably long forest, we can still see her shadow looming over. I still long for the sweets that made me ever so happy. I still long for the sight of her house; a sham on the inside, but outside, a spectacle of its own beauty. Just like the lady who knew what unflinching thoughts lay inside of her? Who knew?

Aditya Mahesh Thakur (15)
ACS Egham International School, Egham

THE PEACH BOY

Long ago, an uncle and aunt lived in the mountains.
One day, Aunt went to the river to wash clothes. While Aunt was there, a peach rolled down from upper stream. She caught it and cut it open. Inside, there was a baby they called Peach Boy, he grew up fast.
When he understood the townspeople were worried about ogres, he walked to the mountain to fight them. On his way to the mountain he acquired servants: a turtle, a fox and a caterpillar who helped him defeat the ogres. After the battle they all lived with Aunt and Uncle.

TOMOAKI HAYASHI (15)
ACS Egham International School, Egham

KOLOBOK

Long, long ago, Kolobok, a little yellow bun, was rolling from Wolf, Bear and Rabbit because all of them wanted to eat him. They followed him all the way through the forest until Kolobok hid in the bush. They passed him without noticing. Once they had gone, Kolobok rolled slower, but then Fox noticed him and said, 'Kolobok, I will eat you!'
While she said this, Wolf, Bear and Rabbit ran back and noticed Kolobok with Fox. Then they shouted, 'Kolobok is mine!' and they all began to fight so Kolobok rolled away from them easily.

ARSLAN RUSLANOV (15)
ACS Egham International School, Egham

IT

I lay there as still as possible while its giant blood-covered fangs dripped on my face, hoping it wouldn't sense my presence. I was so close I could hear its heartbeat and feel its every breath. Then, all of a sudden, it snapped its head down and stared at me as if it was looking into my soul. I slowly pulled out my knife and stabbed it three times, but it was not enough. It simply just picked me up in its giant jaw and thrashed me about from side to side, then it just stopped.

TAYLOR CLARKE (18)
Apple Orchard School, Horsham

THE POWER WITHIN

The day started young and bright. It ended in tragedy. I did not expect to encounter so much trouble. Five men could do nothing.The army could do nothing. I could do nothing. The taste of blood on my lips. The power I could feel flowing through my veins. I knew it would be the end of me and the people I loved if I did not stop. I will never stop! I drink people dry for I am the most feared thing to walk on this Earth, for I am a vampire and I will drink your life form dry.

RYAN NORMAN (16)
Apple Orchard School, Horsham

THE ESCAPE

Sitting alone, in the darkness. Silence, except for scurrying rats. The cold bites my skin as I wait. One chance, just one. Then I'll be free. Heavy footsteps. The scraping of boots on stone. A key rattles in the lock. The door creaks as it swings open. 'Come on then!' he growls. I stand and look at the mouldy bread and dirty water on the metal tray he holds in his hands. 'Eat up!' he says with a smirk. I extend my claws and strike his face. On all fours I run out into the moonlit night. I am free!

CHRISTOPHER CHOWN (17)
Apple Orchard School, Horsham

OBLIVION

My knee cracks painfully as I climb the ladder, reminding me that I'm not the young man I once was. I walk confidently towards the edge of the building, the wind whipping my hair. I'm wearing my old uniform, the one I wore all those years ago, the same one that used to make me feel like such a man, the same one that used to strike fear into the hearts of so many. I take a deep breath, tears blocking my vision now, click my heels together, raise my arm in a salute, lean forward, and tumble into oblivion.

AARON CLARKE (16)
Apple Orchard School, Horsham

THREE STRIKES AND YOU'RE OUT!

It was dark and cold. He reached for the matches, and the matches were put in his hands! He needed light, so he struck the match with his shaking hands. That was the first mistake he made. Then something whispered, 'The cut! The cut!' On the second strike the match lit! As he looked at his arm, 'Death' was carved into his arm! That's what the acute extreme pain was! But the match blew out! The third strike ended with a blood-curdling, bone-breaking scream! He was gone! The killer was found after ten were killed. Ten murder cases!

LEON INGHAM (13)
Apple Orchard School, Horsham

THE WOLF EATER

Once upon a time, there was a little girl who baked cookies for her grandmother.
On a Friday evening, Red was walking to her gran's house. When she got there the door had a red stain. She was intrigued, so she walked in, sat down on the chair next to her gran's bed and fell asleep.
She woke to the noise of a gag. It was her grandmother. Her mouth was covered in the blood of a wild animal. She had just finished devouring a wolf.

SEAN PRICE
Apple Orchard School, Horsham

When Predator Became Prey

The queen, clad in the cloak of night, tore through the tangle of browny green arms. Her skin dressed in thorns and dirt, but everything was forgotten when an arrow seared off her ear. The snow was stained a delicious shade of crimson. Then suddenly there were dwarfs. One in front, and flanking her sides were six more. Behind her poised a huntress; coal-black hair, snow-white skin, rosy red lips. Bow and arrow were tight in her hands, the weapon's tip marked for the heart, 'We used to have a queen,' Snow White sneered, 'once upon a time.'

NARISA LIMPAPASWAT (15)
Bellerbys College, Brighton

Sleeping Ugly And The Unfortunate Prince

Sleeping Ugly was locked in a faraway tower. She was imprisoned because wherever she went plants started to wilt and animals would die in the presence of her ugly face.
One day, a prince stumbled upon the tower while riding through the forest on his unicorn. He got off his unicorn and knocked on the door of the tower. No answer. He broke into the tower and climbed the stairs. At the top of the tower, the prince saw Sleeping Ugly. At the sight of her, the prince had a traumatic seizure and he died. He was very unfortunate.

KAE JUN CHAI (16)
Bellerbys College, Brighton

BROKEN

Being the most remarkable angel among them, jealousy must appear, twisting off her wing had been secretly planned by the other angels for a few years. After the evil plan was completed, they just needed to wait for the perfect moment. Lying on the ground with a terrifyingly pale face, she had no more energy to struggle, the image of what just happened kept replaying in her mind. The ferocious eyes, the bawl, the evil smile, and her ring of light lost. The pair of wings that she used to be so proud of were ripped from her forever.

YU KI HO (17)
Bellerbys College, Brighton

DECEMBER THE NINTH

I come towards the door and I hear you screaming. Suddenly, I see you lying on the floor with half your head gone, the door between us vanishes but I see no blood around you. My heart breaks and tears fall out of my eyes, they all of a sudden turn red, my tears turn red, blood is falling out of my eyes, everything is going dark, everything is disappearing. I am all alone, there is nobody with me, there's nothing here. I hear people laughing, what is happening to me? I forgive you, save me, I am lost.

MOHAMMAD JAWED (15)
Bellerbys College, Brighton

THE GIRL IN THE CLOAK

Her red cloak flutters in the misty forest, white steam comes out from her tiny mouth irregularly. Heavy footsteps echo behind her. They get closer and closer. The ground vibrates. The grass shivers. Dewdrops are on the ground. Hairy palms encircle her slender neck, claws prick into her skin; pure red splashes into the air. The wolf howls; the silence is pierced. Her body stops struggling.

I open my eyes. I'm lying on my bed which reflects the white of the moonlight. I put my hand on my neck to stop the dream stabbing. It's covered with sticky blood.

CHING YANG (16)
Bellerbys College, Brighton

MY PRINCE CHARMLESS

My fingers are trembling, my heart is aching. Isn't it ironic how we use pain to relieve pain? What Prince Charmless did a month ago almost killed me; like a gunshot into my heart. But today was like a replay; I saw him, a smirk on his face, strolling with Little Black Riding Hood. Is she the girl who could finally be good enough for him? However, I stayed on my two feet when he pulled the trigger. It does not hurt any less, I'm just building up my tolerance for pain. My Prince Charmless shall be missed.

BERNICE GOH (16)
Bellerbys College, Brighton

REFLECTION

Charlotte talks to mirrors. They mumble faintly and whisper, as if afraid to speak. Charlotte tells them secrets, like how angry she is and how vile she feels when her parents favour her reflection. All loneliness turns to hurt; from there is born rage, that flourishes in little Charlotte like a storm. Forgotten are her inhibitions. She screams, spits and claws at the mirror, and her reflection wails and bleeds. Charlotte's mind is shattered glass, and with blackened shard she slashes. Charlotte talks to mirrors, real ones now. For her twin sister is dead. And she is truly alone.

MEGAN CLAPSON (16)
Davison CE High School for Girls, Worthing

DEVIL GIRL

There a dark mysterious figure stood in the shadows watching, waiting. She hadn't seen him, he was sure. He inched slowly forward, silent as a corpse. He made a sound, and his heart stopped, but she hadn't seen him. He continued to move more cautiously now though. He saw her whip her head to face in his direction. No! He must have made a sound, but he couldn't remember doing so. He crouched among the ferns, staring at the ground. He waited a moment then stood up. She was gone. He heard a noise. He slowly turned around and screamed.

JESS TAYLOR (13)
Downlands Community School, Hassocks

Juliet's Last Call

Juliet called out once more across Verona's setting sun. 'I'm down here my love,' called Romeo.
'Where?' replied Juliet, in a truly puzzled tone.
Juliet suspected Romeo was out of her sight, so she leaned over the edge a little. She called once more and once again Romeo was answering, but out of sight. Juliet leaned over a little more, and finally she spotted Romeo! 'Why are you standing upside down?' said Juliet. Suddenly there was one scream and one thump!
'You could have used the stairs dear,' said Romeo. Although that fell on dead ears...

JOSHUA HUTCHINSON (13)
Downlands Community School, Hassocks

Twisted

The warm soft lips of the beautiful Prince Charming, delicately press onto the cloud-white cheeks of Snow White. Joy between the two of them as they are finally reunited. They head to their house, happy as ever before. Strange noises of groaning come from the house but it is ignored. Grumpy, the dwarf, with a piercing look of blood dripping down his mouth and scratches all over his body. More and more of the poor dwarfs surround Snow White and her prince. And now the story is over.

TOM YOUNG (13)
Downlands Community School, Hassocks

All For Nothing

Morning, still a little woozy from last night, still missing a shoe, she came downstairs with her cleaning supplies barefoot and started to clean. She went outside and stepped on a stinging nettle and her foot swelled. She then stepped on a broom and foot bled. Knock at the door she hobbled to the door, opened it. It was the guy from last night. He wanted her to try on her shoe. She put it on. *Stuck!* Pus and blood filled the shoe, he tried to pull it off. He fell on a rock and died, without love.

MEGAN CARTER (12)
Downlands Community School, Hassocks

Cinders!

Heard the Cinders' tale? Well this one has a slight twist. Cold, tired, neglected, Cinders was depressed. Thing one and thing two got to go to the ball but she didn't.
She saw a puff of ash and her fairy godmother appeared! She popped her in a tutu and rushed her off to the ball. When she got there her stepsister was dancing but the prince was annoyed and cut her head off.
The day after the prince came around with a slipper. But it didn't fit Cinderella so she chopped half her foot off. The slipper fit.

NATASHA BARTON WALLS (11)
Downlands Community School, Hassocks

Untitled

As Cinderella arrived at the ball, her fairy godmother stopped her and said, 'You could have had it all, but you got paired with me!' With one more flick of her wonderful wand, they were in a dark and empty warehouse. The fairy godmother broke Cinderella's glass slipper and stuck it in her thigh, then dragged it slowly down her leg. All you could hear were the deafening howls in the dead of night.

JOSH ALLEN (13)
Downlands Community School, Hassocks

Snow White And Cinderella's Bloody Tale

An ordinary red ruby apple was handed to her. *Crunch,* she fell into a pit of sharp silver knives.
'Yes!' I cried. 'She's dead. Dwarfs come along now!'
Every limb was torn out and then replaced in the same place. *Creak!* Snow White, not so white now, was placed on the swing in young Cinderella's garden.
Cinderella ran out into the garden where... her head turned. Screaming, surrounded by them, a dozen screams but nobody could hear. *Crunch!* Blood, bones everywhere! Cinderella gone but the swing carried on swinging in the garden, some say she still comes back to haunt.

ELLA-MAY CHANDLER (13)
Downlands Community School, Hassocks

27

Winter Wonderland Or A Forest For Disaster?

Hair as black as coal, skin as white as snow. Snow White was her name. This tale, a bit different to others, is one you'll never forget. Once Snow was in what she called 'Winter Wonderland', but to everyone else a 'Forest for Disaster'.
Suddenly, Snow heard footsteps coming closer. Little men, dwarfs. *Bang!* Snow was dead! Her head rolling down the hill, blood was following its every move.
At the cottage, news spread. Snow's stepmother was so devastated, death was the only way to stop her misery. So she ate a red apple and stabbed herself with a knife.

KATE VICTORIA BARKLEY (12)
Downlands Community School, Hassocks

A Telltale Heart

I walked stealthily into the room. I could see the old man lying in his bed, he was fast asleep. Slowly, I walked over to the cupboard, out of the cupboard, I got the sharp blade that I hid there. I held the blade tightly in my right hand. I walked over to the old man's bed. I plunged the knife into his chest. He had stopped breathing and he had no pulse. Suddenly, he sat up and punched me in the face, he then pulled the blade out of his chest and threw it at my heart!

ROBBIE PAYNE (14)
Downlands Community School, Hassocks

GRANSEL AND HETTLE

Woe be to the children who left their home forcibly. Banished to the forest all alone with only a few stones for company. Cleverly creating a path back to their house with said stones. They left, never to return. They couldn't believe their luck when they found a cottage made entirely out of gingerbread, standing before them! However, out of nowhere a witch jumped out and attacked them! Luckily they threw their stones at the witch and killed her! Happily they tucked into their treat of a house but ate too much and exploded into lots of pieces.

MILES ALFREY (12)
Downlands Community School, Hassocks

THE CREATURE

It started with a whisper. I leapt up shrieking. Was it my dream? No. But then I grew silent for there was a creak coming from the floorboards. I did not dare breathe, for a dark shadow fell onto my face. The creature was creeping towards me, growling and moaning as it did so. The pace of my heartbeat grew louder, louder. Before long the creature was inches from my face, his breath was colder than ice on my cheeks. I tilted my head slowly. However, no creature was there. I was reaching for the poison next to me...

WILL JENKINSON (13)
Downlands Community School, Hassocks

Gods

Thud... Thud... Thud...
My body jumping, darkness consumed my eyes.
Thud...Thud...Thud...
I prayed and pleaded with my mind.
Thud... Thud... Thud...
My body laid still and broken.
'I am death!' a deep, dark voice boomed.
I was in shock and I could not move.
'Did you really think you could escape?'
'No!'
Its voice, so loud, burst my soft ears.
'I could leave you in this void of nothing,' he shrieked, 'but alas, no, enjoy your soul, you won't have it for long,' he chuckled loudly.
Before I knew it, two red arms reached for me, pushing down...

OLIVER TAGARSI (14)
Downlands Community School, Hassocks

The Princess And The Knife

There once was a princess as elegant as can be, the story goes that she lay on a pea, no that's not right. This princess was very fair, she had rosy cheeks and golden hair, she was very thin and extremely small, the perfect size to dance at the ball. The day before she was to meet her prince, her mother politely said, 'A princess needs two things; a nice long sleep and a comfy bed.' So off she went up to her bed, but once she had tucked herself in, a knife emerged through her mattress, into her skin.

ELLIE FINCH (14)
Downlands Community School, Hassocks

THE HUNTSMAN

You all know the tale of the fair maiden with skin as white as snow and hair as black as death, Snow White. Snow's stepmother, the queen, grew jealous of her beauty and tried to kill her in her sleep but the huntsman knew the queen's cunning plan and killed the queen. Snow White was so pure of heart that she blamed herself for her stepmother's death. After a long and painful year tormenting herself with guilt, she took her own life with a shotgun and left her dead body in her room to rot until the end of time.

ZARA NIKOLIC (13)
Downlands Community School, Hassocks

NOCTURNAL NIGHT

The young girl's hour had come. I turned the lambasted latch of the girl's room oh ever so gently. Dexterously, but nonchalantly, I lurked into the room. I stealthily ambled over to her. I couldn't help but observe the young mistress. Oh how beautiful she was. I hesitated for a second. No! I smothered the pillow over her face, but death wasn't upon her. Yet! I withdrew the cold, ductile knife from my sleeve. I started sawing her into little pieces, just so I had a memory of the killing. You shall call me mad. But I'm not!

CALLIE ALLISON (14)
Downlands Community School, Hassocks

Unnatural Selection

There. A streak of grey stood out against the forest. Prince Charming strode towards it, and into a clearing. In the centre stood a massive tower; it had no doors, only a single window high above him. Out of it hung a long golden braid, which he climbed. Upon reaching the window, he saw a beautiful girl smiling at him. However, before he could say anything, her smile turned cold. He watched in horror as she drew a knife and sliced viciously through her braid. The last thing he remembered was the icy wind whipping his face as he fell.

Sophie Simpson (12)
Downlands Community School, Hassocks

Redilocks

The three bears lived in a cottage in the woods, so rarely got any visitors; but, when they did, they liked to make them welcome. Goldilocks was passing by so the bears had company. Daddy Bear gathered ten bloodthirsty hounds from the dog pound. Goldilocks didn't know that her life was going to flash before her eyes. Baby Bear was in disguise. Daddy Bear released the dogs. Goldilocks screamed as she realised she was going to die. She froze, she was paralysed for a moment or two! Goldilocks was not so goldy her hair was blood-red!

Charlee Sadler (13)
Downlands Community School, Hassocks

GOLDILOCKS

It was the eve of September the sixth when Goldilocks, the local hobo, decided she was hungry. Whilst she was snooping around some bins she came across a lovely house with the door wide open. As she walked in, she felt a line of something cross her leg - a trip wire! In the blink of an eye her legs were stumps, blood gushing out, but she was determined to have food. She found three bowls of soup, blood-red, she sat down to try it. Out of nowhere a bear used his claw to finish Goldi off!

TOBY FISHER (12)
Downlands Community School, Hassocks

A NEW SHADE OF RED

Basket in hand, with cookies ready, the girl took off nervous but steady. However she did not win the race. The wolf had a quicker pace. A lick of his lips, a bite of Grandma's head, he quickly scampered into bed! 'Come in, sit down my dear.' But Riding Hood knew and shed a tear. The wolf, wishing for another meal, was ready to leap, pounce and kill. Little Red had the same idea. She had a knife and fork and began to cheer. A cut, a splash, a new shade of red; a wolfskin cloak upon her head.

LYDIA IVES (13)
Downlands Community School, Hassocks

THE EMPEROR'S NEW COAT

There once was an emperor all happy and proud. But placed looks in his heart and soon felt down. Two fine men appeared at his door, offering an outfit of the finest essence known to the lords. Laughing and sniggering, they made a coat of thin air. He sat there watching hour upon hour, not saying a word, just sitting all dour. However, because of jealously the people of Norfolk revolted and killed the king and his relatives, except for one, his youngest son usurped his father and took his position as king.

HOLLY MEREDITH (12)
Downlands Community School, Hassocks

BROKEN ALICE

The hole looks so inviting she knew not what lay beneath but was certain that her curiosity could not be satisfied unless she jumped in. So she bent her knees and launched herself deep, into the dark, never-ending tunnel of mystery. Alice, the girl of beauty, fell further and further, smacking her head on various branches. Blood slithered down her decapitated face as random pieces of her body sprang off of her torso and fell quickly down the unlit tunnel. Blood sprayed everywhere, leaving Alice's shattered corpse on the ground. The hungry Mad Hatter ate it all.

OLIVIA GILL (13)
Downlands Community School, Hassocks

GOODBYE GOLDILOCKS

Goldilocks got home and heard a knock. She went to find out what it was, however she wished she hadn't. On the doorstep there were three dark soul, evil bears. She stared into their hypnotic eyes, they asked her name, she had no power to resist. 'Goldilocks,' she replied.
'Follow us Goldie,' they said.
As they entered, the door slowly closed behind them.
That night the neighbours ran towards the screams. Her door was open, but when they got there, all they could see were drops of blood. Since that horrific day, poor old Goldilocks was never seen again!

ADAM DAVIES (12)
Downlands Community School, Hassocks

THE SEVEN MEN

As a girl went into the woods today, to find somewhere to sleep, she came across a little house, to find herself some treats, she ran upstairs and fell asleep, as seven people heard her squeals, Seven men ran upstairs to find Snow White was there, Snow White woke up, seven men wouldn't shut up, Snow White pulled out a gun and killed the seven men. Snow White had seven new coats.

CHARLOTTE SAUNDERS (13)
Downlands Community School, Hassocks

35

GIRL IN THE WOOD

Once there was a girl wandering through the wood. It was a serene day until a breeze of death brushed her shoulder. A sensation to run made her sprint. Once she came to a clearing she thought she was safe. The silence was deafening. Her heartbeat could be heard from a mile. Until again, the noise: the whisper of death. She ran through the weeds, hoping for safety, her widened eyes darting towards a humble house made of sweets. Abruptly she ran, her pace quickening. Inside she went, until the red eyes met hers. The windows now stained red.

OLIVIA LUCAS (12)
Downlands Community School, Hassocks

SLEEPING DEMON

The prince crept into the silent room. A beautiful young woman with flowing, silky hair met his eyes. He crept slowly over to her four-poster bed. Right before his eyes, he saw her, lifeless. He bent down, tucking her hair behind her ear. As his lips were about to meet hers, the princess' eyes opened to reveal blood trickling. She opened her mouth slightly to show her terrible white teeth, blood dripping. Her hands rose above her head, needle-sharp nails. Suddenly, the prince was no more. Head ripped clean off!
Watch out. She's coming for you too!

OLIVIA MURRAY (11)
Downlands Community School, Hassocks

Rapunzel Retold

Rapunzel sat on her chiselled cold floor, wishing for excitement. Her wicked stepmother flew past and abruptly threw her a note. It said, 'Have your wish girl, I don't give a damn!' Rapunzel wished for her prince. She heard someone walking past, it was her prince. 'Here!' she called. Surprised, he looked up. The prince climbed up her hair. Almost at the top, he called, but no reply. Rapunzel sharpened her silver scissors, *Snip!* He fell to the ground. Rapunzel's laugh sent a shiver spiralling down spines of even the smallest creature.

GEORGIA LANGSTON (12)
Downlands Community School, Hassocks

Cinderella: What Really Happened

There once was a beautiful girl called Cinderella. She lived in a great big house with her stepmother and two sisters. Cinderella was treated like a lowly slave; she was the one that did all the cleaning and cooking and washing and scrubbing.
One day, the family got an invitation from the royal family, inviting them to the regal ball. Cinderella was overjoyed. But her evil stepmother said she had to stay behind and clean. Cinderella was outraged.
So that night Cinderella crept into her stepmother's room, and with one big swoop of her meat cleaver, chopped her head off!

AMY GRACE GELNAR (12)
Downlands Community School, Hassocks

THE DAY THE PRINCE DIED

Asleep on the bed, she looked so calm. Her pink dress simply glowed. He couldn't be satisfied unless he kissed the beautiful stranger who intrigued him to her side. He leaned in, not realising what would happen. 'She looks so inviting,' he said to himself, trying to convince himself it was a good idea. Suddenly, she sat up, reached for her sword and with one clean swish he was beheaded; with five swishes he was completely limbless, just a stump lying on the floor. She picked him up and placed him on her bedside table to preserve for later!

CHLOË-ROSE HODGES (13)
Downlands Community School, Hassocks

MONSTERS WITH THE FACE OF YOUNG

Thump. Thump. My heartbeat quickens with every breath taken. My hands, like the rattling windows, shake uncontrollably. My heart almost stops as thunder claps. Clawing at my sanity. The magic within my blood warns me of ominous danger, fills the rotten air around me with a shadow of death. Suddenly, electric energy illuminates the entire room. They are coming. Instant, irrational fear envelops my soul... *Creaaak.* Slowly, so slowly, I turn to the door. They are here! The two sent to kill me, a good witch of the North Hills! Fiendish witch hunters! It's them... Hansel and Gretel.

CHARLOTTE HODGE (14)
Downlands Community School, Hassocks

Cinderella Updated!

Suddenly, an old cloaked woman appeared out of nowhere and transformed Cinderella's clothes into a shimmering golden dress and sent her to the ball to dance with Prince Charming.
After that night, her stepmother realised that Cinderella was the beautiful girl at the ball and so cut her feet off. When she came to try on the shoe it just fell off, but it sadly fitted Anastasia and so she went to the palace instead. When the prince went to see Anastasia she grabbed a dagger and killed the prince. Ever since she has been locked up in a tower.

Madeleine Grace King (13)
Downlands Community School, Hassocks

The Story Of Snow White

Snow White was young and beautiful until her stepmother came along.
Snow White was knocking on her stepmother's door. The door opened with a high-pitched squeaking and she looked in and there was a head on the floor, she saw her stepmother weeping, the grim prince came from over the wall, he was proud and tall. The stepmother saw him and got annoyed, soon his head would be destroyed. She was jealous and in her mind he was dead, so she used the knife to cut off his head. Her mind was crazy, so she ran away and exploded.

Jasmine Ware (13)
Downlands Community School, Hassocks

Untitled

A little girl skipping through the woods with a red hood, off to her grandma's house.
Meanwhile, at her grandma's house, a blood-curdling wolf is thirsty for blood, stealthily seeking prey as he approaches the old cottage. He enters, sees the old woman lying there and horrifically gobbles her up.
The little girl approaches the ancient cottage unknowing of the danger, she approaches the wolf, she grabs a machete and plunges the knife into the wolf, unaware of her grandma inside. The blade shoots straight through the wolf and into her grandma. Not all stories have a happy ending!

Robert Farley (13)
Downlands Community School, Hassocks

Cinnamon Dreams

The man's hour had come as I lunged forward. He summoned two of the most fluffy and badass unicorns ever, to protect him and his evil eye from its inevitable demise; but I summoned even more fluffy, even more cute and even more badass Shetland ponies! The epic battle that ensued was too cute and too badass to put into words. But what I can say is that the unicorns played dirty by farting cinnamon at the opponents, but the Shetlands played dirtier by lobbing coal at them. As we all know, coal beats cinnamon.

Sam Chard
Downlands Community School, Hassocks

SNOW WHITE

The prince leaned over and kissed Snow White's blood-red lips. Her eyes flickered and were suddenly full of life. The handsome prince helped her up and led her into an isolated clearing surrounded by trees. Poor Snow White was too pure, too innocent to suspect danger.

Out of view, the prince was changing. His shoulders grew hunched, his teeth crooked, his hair turned grey and an ugly wart appeared on his nose. The evil witch smiled a twisted smile and pulled a dagger from her pocket. In one swift motion she stabbed Snow White, scarlet blood poured out of her.

CLAIRE BRONWEN HERBERT (14)
Downlands Community School, Hassocks

THE OLD MAN'S HOUR HAD COME

It was there, lying before me. He lay on the bed, the eye now lay beside him I took a hot poker from the fire, I plunged it into his stomach. He just lay there, he couldn't feel a thing. I then got a sledge hammer and whipped his head clean off. I ran downstairs and grabbed a couple of bottles of whisky. I coated the old man's remains in the lovely alcohol and threw him in the fire. His body slowly dissolved in the ferocious flames.There was occasional spitting from the body acids, and there was death.

WILLIAM GODWIN (14)
Downlands Community School, Hassocks

41

THE EYE

I had to destroy the evil eye veiled in green. The room, thick with darkness, nothing I could see. Stealthily, I crept to the man with the sickening eye. He lay oblivious, asleep. Staring down into the black pool, his heart pounding ferociously. *Stab!* I plunged my knife into his heart. Suddenly, his emerald eye unfolded into a gracious butterfly. I turned pale, eyes widening, I grew with fear. It flew to me, its soft velvet wings brushing my lips. It forced its body inside my mouth, filling my lungs. Silently I fell to the ground, drowning on gentle wings.

HONOR BRYANT (14)
Downlands Community School, Hassocks

VULTURE EYE

The old man's hour had come. As he walked into the gloomy room he wasn't the only one awake. The vulture eye was waiting. The old man was lying there, eyes wide open. He walked ever so cautiously. He grabbed the old man's neck and didn't let go. Alas the old man leaped up; they tossed and turned. The old man grabbed a letter opener lying beside him and sliced the man all over. The man dropped to the floor in a heap. The old man just stared at him, walked over him and out of the bedroom door.

CHARLOTTE BATES
Downlands Community School, Hassocks

UNTITLED

As I opened the door to the old man's room, I crept in with my lantern dimmed down so I could only see right in front of me. I saw him. I saw him lying there out cold, but I could still hear his heart, *thump, thump, thump*. I didn't like this man, he was cruel and mean. I got an urge to do something. I threw the lantern, just missing him. The man woke and yelled out. He reached out for the lantern and smashed it and hit me in the head, I fell into a blazing fire.

ISABELLA SCORER
Downlands Community School, Hassocks

TELLTALE HEART

There once was a man that I despised. It was not of his actions, it was his eye. Stealthily, stealthily I crept up the stairs. Stealthily, stealthily I had to take care. I reached the room. Opening the door, it screeched and I panicked even more. The lantern or the pillow which was the prize? I chose the lantern: he would meet his demise. Nervously, oh so nervously, I ended his life, but he was a fighter, he too had a knife. The man stood up with his dagger-like knife; he had pierced my heart; there went my life.

BRANDON HAYLOR (14)
Downlands Community School, Hassocks

BOB AND BETH

Have you heard of Jack and Jill? Well I have put a bit of a twist on it.
Bob and Beth went up the mountain to fetch a bucket of poison.
They came skiing down, sleighing down, bobsleighing down. Bob
broke his head, Beth tripped and drank the poison and neither lived
again.

ARCHIE HENDERSON (11)
Downlands Community School, Hassocks

SNOW WHITE AND
THE EVIL QUEEN

Have you heard the true story of Snow White? No?
Snow White's mother died giving birth. Her father, the king, married a
beautiful woman. She, my reader, was pure evil. She treated Snowy
horrifically, so horrifically in fact, Snowy ran away! The evil queen
sent a huntsman to rip out her heart. The huntsman, who loved Snow
White, couldn't do the dirty work, so he and Snowy decided to kill the
evil queen. That night, they broke into the palace and slit her throat
while she slept. They cremated her body the next day. On that day
they wed.

TOM VARLEY (11)
Downlands Community School, Hassocks

Little Red Vampire

So Little Red Riding Hood set off into the forest to collect some apples for her grandma.
Suddenly, Little Red Riding Hood fell to the ground. An ear-piercing scream filled the forest. Then. Silence. Then an eerie voice started to rise from the ground. Blood poured from the girl's sharp teeth. Her head started to break off, her eyes became hollow. She had a poisonous apple in her hand. 'Here you go Grandma,' the little girl cackled. Grandma took one bite of the apple and...

Hattie Payne
Downlands Community School, Hassocks

No Goldilocks And The Three Bears

Once in the dark, mysterious woods, there lived three bears, Mamma, Papa and Baby.
One gloomy morning, they went for a walk into the woods. But Baby was worried that someone would break in!
'What if someone was to burgle us?' he squeaked fearfully.
'Don't worry we'll lay some porridge out on the table and add drops of *flavouring*,' Mamma grinned. 'If they break in they'll eat the porridge and, well, you'll see.'
When they returned they discovered a little girl sat with her head down on the table. She was dead!

Paloma Radley-Smith (12)
Downlands Community School, Hassocks

Midnight Heartbreak

Cinderella slowed down, mud splattered over her shoe, her house was near, and she ached for rest. The stars twinkled around her. She felt light and her entire life seemed brighter. She even wanted to treat her sisters, something so rare before it was impossible. Hopefully Prince Charming didn't mind her running off. As she approached the door, she could hear bedsprings creaking, puzzled, she opened the door. What befell her eyes turned her heart black. The figures seemed to ignore her, moving forward and back. As she picked up the knife, she realised she was quite peckish.

Luca Brett-Smith (13)
Downlands Community School, Hassocks

Untitled

She lay there in her beautiful chair, painfully waiting for her true love to come and rescue her. Suddenly her decadent ears noticed a faraway cry of, 'Rapunzel, Rapunzel let your hair down!'
She jumped up with happiness and yelled down, 'Go away you idiot.'
But then she realised it was the man she was waiting for, her true love. She then let her hair down and screeched, 'Climb up please.'
He shouted back, 'You're dead mate.' And yanked on her hair. She splattered onto the floor and that's why she needed to go to the hairdressers.

Bill Sibun (12)
Downlands Community School, Hassocks

THE ESCAPE FROM THE BEAST

I ran as fast as I could, trying to get away from the beast with it's bright red eyes and thick black fur covering its ginormous body. Every time I'd look behind me it got closer and closer until it was as close as the skin of my teeth. I started to lose my breath as the beast could run for miles more. I could tell it would never give up by the look on its vicious face, growling at me, so I had no choice. Suddenly there was a pitch-black hole, so I jumped for safety.

WILLIAM MANLEY (12)
Downlands Community School, Hassocks

THE BURNT PRINCESS

'Rapunzel! Let down your hair!' Rapunzel looked out of her window to see her prince smiling up at her. In one quick motion she flung her hair out of the window and waited. She felt a pulling and suddenly she found herself falling. The prince had pulled her hair so hard that she had fallen out of the window, into a pit of molten metal. The prince laughed as he watched Rapunzel scream and fry to her death. He then ate the burnt princess with a side of potato smiley faces and a green tea.

ELOISE PRITCHARDS (13)
Downlands Community School, Hassocks

BLEEDING BEAUTY

Slowly treading towards the silhouetted object mysteriously placed in the middle of the vacant room, Aurora is still in a profound trance. As she gets closer to the object, it becomes clear enough to make out a spinning wheel with a stool conveniently placed next to it. Getting closer, her eyes lose focus and she starts to stumble, which causes her to trip over the stool, sending the spike of the spinning wheel straight through her eyeball. It pops and oozes black liquid and blood. She squirms about causing the spike to mash up her retina and kill her instantly.

TOM YELLAND (13)
Downlands Community School, Hassocks

SCARED

I was standing in the woods. It was dark, and there was a low-lying mist. It all looked very sinister, like a scene for a horror movie. I was wearing a long white dress; there was a bridal look about it. The wind whistled through the trees. There was a whimpering. I looked down and there was a wolf. It looked scared of me, but shouldn't it be the other way around? A little girl screamed. I advanced towards her to try and comfort her, but she backed away, even more scared. Why was everything scared of me?

MEDDI ORAM (14)
Farlington School, Horsham

Madame Lalaurie

There once was a beautiful girl named Amanda, the same age as you. She'd a love for horror but never thought any of it was real, until one night when she was reading a story about Madam Lalaurie that she realised all this horror might not be good for her. Madam Lalaurie was an elegant mistress who used to gruesomely murder young girls then use their blood in an attempt to restore her youth and beauty. Then a voice creaked from the cupboard, 'What a beautiful young lady you are. If only I could be as stunning as you.'

Sahara Coles (13)
Farlington School, Horsham

The Night

She stepped out of her house. Power cut, again. She pulled her jacket tighter to her. Ciara knew her mother would hate her going to the shops late at night. Still, she set off into the darkness. But, just outside the shop door, she stopped. A rustle of leaves, Ciara turned to where the noise came from. Nothing. After she collected the matches, she started making her way home. Curious, Ciara wandered off the path. It felt like something was there; she gave up and trudged home. She did not realise that the night was still waiting to pounce!

Anouska De Bruijn (13)
Farlington School, Horsham

The River Mystery

Slowly up the river came the boat, so small only one man could fit in it. Suddenly, *splash!* Something very large slid into the water. Silence filled my ears. *Crack!* The boat broke and the man fell into the water 'Help!' he screamed. I bolted to the nearest town but no lights were on. I knocked on every door until I found someone who owned a boat. In the morning I went back to the place where everything had happened. All that was left was a couple of splinters. The creature, whatever it was, had vanished.

LAUREN ELLIOTT (13)
Farlington School, Horsham

The Possessor

As the red cloak flew away into the wind, Ruby cried out in pain. Her body was changing! Arms, legs, fingers, even her back were moving in the wrong direction. She was only a girl. She didn't want to become a beast. There! The beast! It was haunting her, becoming her. Suddenly, all Ruby cared about was meat, raw flesh between her deadly teeth.
Dark trees were closing in on her. It was finished, the transaction was complete. She'd become her worst nightmare, the deadliest creature known to Man, she had become a creature with blood-red eyes and teeth!

RIA HUCK (13)
Farlington School, Horsham

WELCOME TO FEARSOME FOREST

The crimson liquid dripped down his pale arm. Another scratch. His feet were working as hard as they possibly could; his bones were on the brink of shattering. He'd always feared this moment; the scene was the same but his fear way beyond his wildest nightmares. He was a victim. Prey. His catcher's face was contorted with a thirst for blood. His mission - kill the boy. At all costs. The goblin pushed and pushed. Until finally… silence. All that was left, was the body of a helpless boy, lying still in the fearsome forest.

MADDIE RYAN (13)
Farlington School, Horsham

RAPUNZEL

As the prince rode towards the bottom of the tower, Rapunzel gazed out of the window, seconds later she tossed her hair over the side of the tower and the prince climbed up. She greeted him with a huge smile and a big hug, then led him to the centre of the room. 'Close your eyes, I have a surprise for you,' she whispered.
Awestruck by her beauty, he shut his eyes and soon lay dead on the tiled floor!

MOLLY CAVANAGH (13)
Greenfields School, Forest Row

THE BEAST INSIDE

A tearful ballerina, twirling mournfully, violent flames tearing her brittle body apart until her soul weeps as embers. Collapsed on my knees, I cradle the silver dagger close to my heart, as if it is a newborn child. Destined to death. The ruby-encrusted blade chills my blood, the crimson stain along its glossy edge matting my already tangled fur as a desperate tear flees the gloomy prison it's been held captive inside for so long; more and more follow, clouding the sight before me. The lifeless corpse of my sweet princess; her throat slit just like my heart.

ANISE ENDERSBY (13)
Greenshaw High School, Sutton

ALADDIN SEEKS REVENGE ON GENIE

Seeking revenge after my horrifying, terrifying experience in this casket. The inside tremendously dingy from my stinky home. Beneath the old, disrupting bed of mine, rats huddle and gather up food from this horrible, distinctive casket. I'm tired of my life trapped inside with nothing to do, every single day. Over time more fury gathering in me. Surprisingly that day someone picked that lamp and shook it vigorously. I attacked him with authority and frightened him away. 'Ha,' I shouted with evil intentions and thought to myself whether to continue to terrify people. Yes! Who's next?

UMAIR AHMED MUNIR (14)
Greenshaw High School, Sutton

HOW WICKED TALES COME TO BE

Once there was a poet from a distant land, hailing from a country which gifted him with a tongue of most beautiful sounds. The poet travelled across foreign lands so that others may listen with awe to his epic tales of old.

One day, he found an old woman by the roadside, and in kindness began to recite the lullabies of his people with soothing tones. But the old woman despised his voice and so cursed him. Tales began to rot on his tongue, twisting into hate and murder, pillage and rape. He became the father of the bad tales.

ANNA LEA-PAUL (15)
Hurstpierpoint College Senior, Hassocks

THE RED WOLF

The hunters were after me. My feet imprinted in the snow as I looked beyond the starry night.

I looked up at the glistening moon, I heard the voices behind as they got closer and closer... I had no choice. I took off my red hood as it sank into the snow. I kept my eyes on the moon as they turned from dark brown to blood-red. My body twisted and changed into a figure like no other as the hunters stopped and stared at me. As my eyes shone bright, I howled and went in for the kill.

GRACE WALLACE (15)
Limpsfield Grange School, Oxted

BIRD GIRL

A flash of auburn red passed my eyes. A robin. The tiny bird sat on a thin branch chirping. My mind wondered... *How could a bird sit on such a thin branch? Why didn't it snap? How did they fly?*
Suddenly, a bright light blinded me, everything was different. I was up high but my parents were so big. I looked down at myself. I gasped, I was a robin!
I spread my wings, jumped and... flew!
It was incredible. The wind blew through my feathers, making me feel free. I never wanted to go back to my parents again!

KESIA SYMCOX (13)
Limpsfield Grange School, Oxted

THE TOWER AND THE FOREST

Rapunzel is singing. A handsome prince hears her. In the shadows a lone, pale vampire with blood-red eyes stands watching. The prince meets Rapunzel. They fall in love. Dame Gothel is angry, cuts off Rapunzel's hair and sends her to the swamp. Dame Gothel tricks the prince. He is blinded by thorns.
The vampire seizes the prince. Fangs cutting. Howls of pain. Blood flowing. The vampire drinks.
The paler, faster, stronger prince finds Rapunzel. She is confused. He explains. They want to be together forever. He bites her. They leave the swamp. The forest is empty. Everyone is dead.

EMMA SENIOR (15)
Limpsfield Grange School, Oxted

Jack And Jill's Unusual Day

Jack and Jill went up the hill to fetch a bucket of water. Jack fell down the well and Jill came falling after. The well was full of water. Jill swam down to the bottom and found a rusty key. She picked it up and swam to the top to show Jack. Jack swam down and saw a door. He went back up to get Jill. They both opened the door. They turned around and saw a flying carpet. 'What's going on?' they cried. They couldn't get home. They were stuck there forever.

EVIE REDDICK (14)
Limpsfield Grange School, Oxted

Wolf

Two friends became rivals. Same species, same animal. Same strengths and weaknesses. Both almost indestructible. Pretty much the best of the pack. Running, running they went. Battling their hearts out. Fighting for their lives. The she-wolf's alpha testing each move. It was close, very close. Too close. The loser would feel humiliation. The winner would be showered with champagne. But, whatever happened, it was not the end of the fight. Running in the woods together as friendly rivals over the next few years. Running, running they went into the cold, harsh winters. Running, running they went into the mist.

SKYLOUISE RUDDICK (14)
Limpsfield Grange School, Oxted

THE RING'S MISSION

A ring, rose-gold and strong. It fitted Jenny's finger perfectly. At night, when the ring was taken off, it ran through the dark house and out of the door. It saw the target. It ran after the robber. When it got close to the robber it struck. The ring beat him up. The robber ran off, scared. The ring walked back to the house proudly. It went through the big black door and onto the bedside table, recharging its energy for the next dangerous mission that awaited. It couldn't wait for its next mission. It dreamed of the amazing future.

MAYA LAWLER (13)
Limpsfield Grange School, Oxted

THE GOLDEN DRAGON

There used to be a land where the golden dragons roamed free. They were worshipped like gods. A man named Harry ruled over the country, but when he died a new king was crowned. He didn't like dragons and didn't worship, so he had them all killed except for one. A boy found the dragon's egg and looked after it. When it was born and grown up, the dragon fought back at the king. The king fled and a new fantastic king ruled over the kingdom. Dragons were worshipped again. Everyone was happy once more.

TIFFANY MCKAY (13)
Limpsfield Grange School, Oxted

CINDERELLA'S DEEP SLEEP

A lonely homeless girl called Cinderella lived alone in the dark forest. Every day she collected water from a well. It was a long, scary walk. Trees hissed and muttered cruelly as she walked by. Crossing a rickety bridge, some of the wood fell off. One bridge went high over the river. She drank some water and with one sip, she fell to the floor and into a deep sleep. As she fell, out of the corner of her eye she saw a sign saying: *Please do not drink this water, it's poisonous. Love, the Ugly Sisters!*

KATE BAKER (12)
Limpsfield Grange School, Oxted

THE SEARCH FOR A BODY

A bright red, glistening pool of blood surrounded the cafe floor. Next to it, an amputated limb lay abandoned. The owner of the arm was nowhere to be seen, but there was an incriminating trail of blood and coffee. The trail led to a deserted building. The windows had been smashed and the door was a pile of ash. The body wasn't in the building but the body and the coffee had stopped. Nobody knew that the corpse was in the cafe freezer the whole time. His school blazer was draped over him, while his phone played eerie music.

SHEANA TAYLOR (15)
Limpsfield Grange School, Oxted

My Wicked Silhouette

Malicious, feisty, vicious, deadly, dangerous. All the horrendous names you can think of. The perfect description of my inner-self. You see, a part of me is possessed. That part, is what I call 'my true self'. I hate showing it, but now it's taken a turn for the worse. I have been unleashed. Full of detest and frustration. I summoned up the courage to plead for my pathetic life to be spared. My body is disintegrating bit by bit, slowly and painfully. My time has come, I know. My conscience runs cold. Suffocated. I fade into darkness.

Freya Russell (15)
Limpsfield Grange School, Oxted

Mistake

'Leave me alone,' I kept repeating. I was walking home alone when he came. I didn't think taking a short cut home through the dark woods would anger such a beast. When he found me, he stabbed my stomach with one of his dagger-like hands. He let me go... Why? I was running now, swerving past bone-like trees. Adrenalin coursing around my body blinded me of my pain and bleeding wound until I collapsed. I felt like my skin was on fire. I then saw my pursuer stalking towards me, with a shark-toothed Cheshire cat grin...

Cheska Trigg (16)
Limpsfield Grange School, Oxted

THE MIST THAT NEVER DIES

There once was a charming prince who rode with his stallion every day and every night.
One day, he approached a stable full of beautiful horses and spotted a beautiful young girl. He became distracted by her beauty. Meanwhile, the stable owner was casting an evil spell on his horse as the couple said goodbye. The charming prince rode along the decrepit path into the distance. Something didn't feel right - the horse's eyes turned a blood-curdling red. A mist appeared and the horse galloped into the sinister mist. He screamed, fearing for his life. He was gone forever.

NICOLE WIBLIN (14)
Limpsfield Grange School, Oxted

LOU'S EXECUTION

Shaking. Shivering. Blood, dripping. Waiting, waiting, waiting... Sweat pouring. Mind focused on memories, leaving without saying goodbye. Sword slicing my arm, the gang smiling smugly. Tensions rising, anxiety building. Last cuddle, friends held hostage. Final blow drawing close. 'This is it Lou.' Oh no... 'Find words Lou.' I can't speak. The wolf bite was agonising. Posters of my worst nightmare, the clown, are everywhere. What is the value of my life? The axe is ready. My head is compressed, filled with loving emotion. Goodbye world. Swinging, swinging, swinging. The head flies. I'm gone, forever.

ELLIE MAIR (15)
Limpsfield Grange School, Oxted

A Dark Destiny

Falling. Falling through an eternity of flightless space into the depths of Hell. Her name, Maggie. Of only five, so innocent and pure. Without remote knowledge assaulted by her fate. Eyes once blue tainted with black. This was a painless torture as she was happily devoured by her dark destiny. As the sinister masquerade of darkness enclosed on Maggie, she stood lifeless as a mannequin and grinned. Heart beating no longer. A void of darkness eating away at her, leaving the empty shell of a once living child. A silent gust blew and the ashes of Maggie humbly followed.

MÁIRE MCCARRAHER (14)
Limpsfield Grange School, Oxted

A Perfect Storm

By the time the wolf had reached the third pig's house, he was desperate. He knocked rapidly on the front door. 'Let me in!' he cried.
'Yeah right,' yelled the smallest pig.
'As if,' taunted another.
The wolf took a deep breath, trying to calm himself. 'Let me in,' he begged.
'No!' the three pigs screamed in unison.
Defeated, the wolf fled to the hills. Dark clouds surrounded the brick house. Suddenly, the clouds burst, flooding the land. The wolf looked back at the destroyed house. 'I was only trying to warn them,' he muttered, 'I turned vegetarian years ago.'

SOPHIA KLEMENT (15)
Limpsfield Grange School, Oxted

HUMPTY'S DEAD

Alcohol. Antibacterial. Sterilisation. Everything around me. *Beep...* It keeps me alive. *Beep...* I cannot move. Quadriplegia. That's what the doctors call it. *Beep...* I'm not alone, my wife sits opposite. Yet, I still feel alone. I need help eating, washing, breathing, even going to the toilet. My wife is leaving. To get a snack, she says. A couple of minutes, she says. She's gone. Alone again. Helpless. *Beep...* There's a man coming. I pretend to be asleep. Still... Frightened... He comes closer, breathing loud. Leaning towards me pulls, 'Gasp!' and walks out. My death - caused by one fall.

LUCY BARKER (15)
Limpsfield Grange School, Oxted

CINDERELLA 2

Cinderella's new life was a life-lasting reward after the cruelty experienced. Cinderella promised to remember the Godmother, her saviour.
Not knowing Cinderella had left, the Godmother paid her a visit. Shock for the stepmother - the person who aided Cinderella. She longed to take revenge. Plunging at her she grabbed the wand and cursed her. Lunging down the hallway... 'Carriage. Ready. Now!' She wouldn't let Cinderella live a second longer.
Arriving at Cinderella's chamber, let in by the guards, she disguised herself using a charm and hid Cinderella away. The prince fell for it. Now she could take her revenge...

AREEBA AZEEM
Oasis Academy Shirley Park, Croydon

THE ATTIC

I'd always known there was something lurking in the attic. I could sometimes hear a soft whimper or sigh but I would always ignore it. I had too many worries and thoughts on my mind. However, one day my sudden curiosity got the better of me. I lay awake thinking until I heard the soft, yet silvery murmur of the unknown. Stepping out of my bed, I tiptoed past my sister and pulled the door that led to the attic down. Excitement rushed through my blood as I went up the stairs. All of a sudden... darkness.

IRIA BALADO (12)
Oasis Academy Shirley Park, Croydon

THE GIRL IN THE MIRROR

I see the girl looking at me, she looks so different. Her eyes black as night. I used to see the plain girl in the mirror, until today. Past the Devil's face, I saw a sweet girl called Layla John. A normal girl. A normal life. 'Why has she not listened?' the monster grinned with delight. See, Layla was not alone, downstairs was a room full of family and friends. The girl in the mirror stopped smiling, for she too still shared the same mind as Layla. She opened the door, the girl in the mirror went downstairs...

SAMANTHA BLACKWOOD (12)
Oasis Academy Shirley Park, Croydon

THREE BILLY GOATS

One day, Little Red Riding Hood asked the Wicked Witch (AKA Mother) if she could go to her friend's party. She said yes, so she went across the street where the party was. On the way she saw a bridge. As she went across she heard a growl. There were three goats. The first goat jumped up and tried to eat her but she pushed it off. Then, the second one came and she pushed him off. Just as she thought they were gone, the biggest one jumped out and she ran. She couldn't fight them so she got eaten.

CHANELLE MILLER (12)
Oasis Academy Shirley Park, Croydon

LEAD ME

I hovered, contemplating whether I should walk to the wardrobe or not. As I walked towards it, a hushed whisper occurred. Gently reaching out my palm, I twisted the doorknob. Dripping red as hell, fiery as blood, a note of death awaited me. Devastatingly deceiving words lured me. They said: 'Lead me, lead me to the forest where green flusters bright. Lead me, lead me to the tree where bark glistens in the moonlight. Lead me, lead me to the river, the river of blood. Lead me, lead me to my death in day or night!'.

PHENICIA THOMPSON (12)
Oasis Academy Shirley Park, Croydon

Orangella

Her father died. Each day her stepmother and stepsisters controlled her. She was a slave and a servant. She went to the ball. She danced with a prince. She fled at midnight and lost her slipper, her orange peeled slipper! Disappearing into the dark night, she ran. The prince came the next day. He tried the orange slipper on Orangella's orange foot. He kissed her tangy-flavoured lips and felt a tingle. The next day they were wed. They had orange juice. Three children were born. Strawbella, Lemonella and Grapella. Every day from then was a fruity pleasure!

Amy-Janet Ola (12)
Old Palace of John Whitgift School, Croydon

Lunchtime

Waiting. Not knowing if death was upon her or if she was still stuck in a dream. The menacing shadows towered over her as she looked into their intimidating eyes. But she still lay there with no sense of fear. Without any emotion, she got out of the bed and slowly ambled downstairs. The monsters growled with anger. Step by step, she walked downstairs. The creatures followed her. As her stomach rumbled, she turned around. Hungry. At that moment, the monsters stopped. She was ready for lunch. Goldilocks left the bear's house. A girl's favourite meal, three bear stew!

Olivia Faria (11)
Old Palace of John Whitgift School, Croydon

THE PHONE CALL

The girl sat on the blood-red sofa. She was waiting for a friend to come around. Her parents had gone on a holiday. She switched on the television. The phone rang. She went to answer the call. 'Open the door.' There was a knock from the door. She disconnected the call and tried to calm down. The phone rang again. 'I am coming in. Three, two, one... ' The girl froze. The door slowly swung open. She could have died of fear when she saw the tall shadow of a man. Petrified, she ran, with no place to hide...

ALIA JAN (11)
Old Palace of John Whitgift School, Croydon

THE CANDY KILLER

Perched on the hill, the house sat quietly. They moved forward only to hear the sound of their breath. It was long after they reached the house, an old lady sat by the fire. She resembled a witch, they thought. She gave them plenty of candy and a place to stay. However, they began to realise she was no ordinary woman. Hanging up on the wall were pictures of children, mixed expressions on their faces. Things became more clear. This woman was a child murderer and she was out on the hunt for new prey. Were the children too late?

ANEESA JARRAL (12)
Old Palace of John Whitgift School, Croydon

THE QUEEN

The attractive, sympathetic queen, Cinderella, walked towards the two stepsisters who were on the floor scrubbing like they had no more work to do. The queen stared. Went closer. Cinderella gave them a bowl of food to share. They were glad.
One day, Cinderella got an invitation to a ball with the prince. Cinderella was excited. She put on her best dress, then left. The stepsisters were jealous. They took one of Cinderella's dresses, wore it, then went to the ball. Cinderella was so happy she forgot the time. She ran back home. It was a pleasure for her!

SHAARUKA KUNALAN (12)
Old Palace of John Whitgift School, Croydon

TRICKED

The giant saw red. He peered at the imp-like creature emerging from the deep recesses of his massive chair. A boy in fact, with insolence, impudence and greed written all over his face. He had seen it all before... The boy began to strum the golden harp. The giant nodded, eyes nonchalantly closing. The boy smiled with glee, edging his way towards the door. Alas, he did not get far. One of the giant's tenacious arms swept down, knocking him down. Then, with one final thump of the giant's shoe, the boy was no more. Snuffed out just like that.

SHREYA JOHN (11)
Old Palace Of John Whitgift School, Croydon

FATAL FRUIT

Darkness enveloped the scene. Any joy or happiness had been sucked out of the atmosphere and was replaced with despair and fears. Fear that the princess would never wake up. Shivers ran down the spectators' spines. They watched the dear girl with trepidation. Death was a sleepless malice, never resting, constantly eating away at her soul. A deadly menace devouring its victim. A lethal predator and its helpless prey. The girl's soul had diminished and her body would decay and she would pass into the abyss. All that would remain of her was mere memory, just like the apple.

OLIVIA LEDGER (11)
Old Palace Of John Whitgift School, Croydon

UNLUCKY

She knew five was unlucky when the clock struck 5am. She ran out only to find sweetcorn on the porch. The midnight-black horses were now only tiny figurines. The waves lashed against the walls of the castle. Each wave got bigger and bigger. Suddenly, a huge wave poured over her. She cursed the sea, knowing she couldn't go home like this. She tried walking but tripped, her shoe falling off her foot. The shoe clip-clopped down the staircase. Suddenly, it stopped on the second to last step. She turned. A shadow stood in the doorway. Unlucky!

AIMIE ELIANE KORN (12)
Old Palace Of John Whitgift School, Croydon

THE DISAPPEARANCE

No one wanted her here. It didn't matter whatever it took, Snow White would disappear like mist dissolving into thin air. *Thud! What was that noise?* In the corner of her eye, she saw a pitch-black figure. *Who was it? What was it?* A shiver ran down Snow White's spine. Sweat trickled down her forehead. Run! That word repeated itself in her head. She froze still. Mysteriously, that sly man didn't move either. Like a lightning bolt, Snow White took off, the bulky man at her heels. Snow White would go, and that was for sure.

KHUSHI ANAND (11)
Old Palace Of John Whitgift School, Croydon

GOODBYE TO THE FAIREST OF THEM ALL

She stood there. Alone. The woman circled her. The girl's pale skin trickled with sweat and fear. The woman drew closer. The girl screamed and ran. Where could she go? The fairest of them all had nowhere to run. The woman would hunt her down. She had to be the fairest of them all. Screams of the girl echoed over the dark night in the lonely forest. The beautiful woman retreated back to her castle. She would think of another way to get her.

HANNAH BOYCE (12)
Old Palace Of John Whitgift School, Croydon

ROCKERELLA

Rockerella entered the rock concert, knowing her limited time was 3am. She jumped her way in rhythm to the music. After the festival of loudness, she went backstage and met one of the bass players. They rocked and danced together all night long, losing time. Whilst she was dancing, she saw a clock in the corner of her eye, and saw it was 2:59am! She let go of the player's hands and ran into the night, leaving behind her autographed CD and the handsome bass player clueless.

EUGENIE BYRON (11)
Old Palace Of John Whitgift School, Croydon

TRICKS, NO TREATS!

Now here is the real story, I never liked Gretel, no one did, not even my dad. Gretel was given to us when my auntie died. We hated her all along... I knew the way home, but Gretel didn't. When dropping the bread, I knew it would be gone when we came home, thanks to the birds. The old woman was in on it too. I was eating candy and pretending to work, while Gretel was working hard. Into the fiery cauldron...I can still remember the screams!

SARAH ZAINAB SHEIKH (12)
Old Palace Of John Whitgift School, Croydon

69

TRAPPED

She was trapped. Alone. Thrown out of her castle, she ran, scared, in a new world. The woods, dark and abandoned, no one was around. Menacing sounds echoed through the tall trees and then she saw it. A hut. She walked closer and closer. A pair of eyes lit up. Two, three, seven pairs glaring at her. They lit up, glowing closer and closer. She couldn't do anything, her blood-curdling screams the only sound around. She ran and never looked back.

ANOUSHKA SAMANTA (11)
Old Palace Of John Whitgift School, Croydon

THE DOUBLE FALL

The woods. That's where the girl was picking up flowers for her grandma. She stopped. She heard a grizzling noise. It was a wolf.
'Hello,' he said. 'Where are you going?'
'To my grandma's. She lives in the cottage at the end of this path.'
The wolf followed the path. 'Grandma?' the girl knocked.
'Come in.'
'Grandma! This doesn't look like you!'
'It is.' The girl threw the covers and saw it was the wolf! She got something sharp. The wolf fell and so did her grandma!
'Oh my, what have I done?' There was nothing but complete, utter silence.

KAMILLE ARCHER (12)
Old Palace Of John Whitgift School, Croydon

WAY, WAY WORSE

The girl was sleeping. Such a beauty, a flawless child. Time to stop that. The prince walked up to her, bent down and planted a kiss. She was revived, only to die again. The prince cackled, 'My mother cursed you but I, I'm going to do something much worse!' Lightning struck and muffled screams echoed throughout the palace walls. The prince grinned. His laugh was piercing, daring. One last striking scream escaped Beauty's soft, red lips. The castle was now silent, except for the laughs. 'Way, way worse!' he whispered.

SABRINA CHOUDARY (11)
Old Palace Of John Whitgift School, Croydon

TIME GOES BY...

Prick. The fair girl slowly fell asleep. Unhappiness spread across the castle. Evil witch Maleficent's curse had finally come true. The 16-year-old had fallen asleep for 100 years. Year later, an explorer passed by seeing the sombre castle and decided to investigate. The explorer sought Sleeping Beauty. A kiss. She awoke. But in agony she screamed. Wrinkles appeared all over her. She had aged. The 16-year-old had turned 40. The explorer ran away in disgust. Poor Sleeping Beauty lived unhappily single ever after.

LYDIA BAVANANTHAN (12)
Old Palace Of John Whitgift School, Croydon

THE DISAPPEARANCE

Why did they have to leave their home to go to the forest? That's where they walked until they saw a small cottage which seemed to be made of sweets. There. A flash of light. A witch appeared. They walked towards the cottage, showing no sign of fear. They stopped, not knowing what to do next. They took a sweet. Ate it. The witch cackled. They turned to meet her eyes. Instantly, something happened. A strange sight. Beasts? The witch had turned them into beasts! They ran, not knowing where to go next. The witch cackled again. Then she disappeared.

DEMI BAKO (12)
Old Palace Of John Whitgift School, Croydon

THE MIDNIGHT BALL

'Once upon a time,' that's how they go, this one might be different... A beautiful girl, Cinderella, was at a forbidden ball. She was told not to go! Cinderella danced with the handsome prince, but she feared he was hiding something under his mask. Was it his face? Soon enough, the clock spoke its words. Seconds later, Cinderella was wearing her rags. Maybe she should have just listened to her stepmother. Her eyes suddenly focused onto the 'handsome' prince. He wore similar clothes to Cinderella. The prince fled from the ball. Cinderella ran. Her mask bounced onto the dance floor.

ANUSHKA THAPLIYAL (12)
Old Palace Of John Whitgift School, Croydon

JACK AND THE GIANT

He was finally there, at the top of the beanstalk. The largest door Jack had ever seen appeared. A gush of water shaped like a teardrop fell onto Jack. He heard whimpering. Where did that noise come from? There was a huge giant. 'I'm lonely, can you stay with me?' he cried.
Jack replied, 'Absolutely not, I have to get back to my mother.'
The giant roared, dragged Jack and locked him in a filthy old cell. The giant grabbed an axe and cut down the beanstalk. Jack would never be able to return to his mother ever again.

AAMILAH MIRZA (12)
Old Palace Of John Whitgift School, Croydon

HAPPILY EVER AFTER?

He galloped on his magnificent snow-white stallion through the mysterious forest, not knowing where, until he reached a tall, sinister stone tower. A glossy golden plait tumbled down from the heavens. Seizing the plait, he climbed and climbed, his limbs aching, his heart pounding. At last he reached a narrow window. A young woman stood, her azure eyes flashing with a sour look. Stepping forward, she shoved him off the window ledge and he hurtled down, down, landing in a bed of cruel, prickly thorns. Darkness. He couldn't see, blinded by the thorns.

CHARLOTTE WATKINS (11)
Old Palace Of John Whitgift School, Croydon

The Twisted Door

Rainy, bitter and wet. Fighting the angry showers, he knocked on the big oak door. She glanced at him with eyes as black as the night, *could he be the one?* Carefully, she planned a sleepless night full of terrors. *Would he still be there at the break of dawn?* He tossed and he turned, cursing the path that had led him there. Enough was enough! Ignoring the wind and the creaks of the floor, he set off to find the big oak door. Away he went to his comfortable bed. Whilst the princess turned her lonely, miserable, downcast head.

ISOBEL SMITH (12)
Old Palace Of John Whitgift School, Croydon

The Man In The Black Coat

The man in the black coat seemed suspicious, but I never thought he would lead me to this; The Frankenstein of food! He said, 'Just add a drop to your dough, your baking will come alive!' Who knew he meant it? I was half my age and I only wanted to win the National Baking Competition. That was just twenty years ago and now, at forty, what happened to that terrorising ginger biscuit is still a mystery. I never saw the man again and the world still doesn't know the real story of the Gingerbread Man.

JULIETA CANI (12)
Old Palace of John Whitgift School, Croydon

LOST IN THE FIELDS

Walking. More walking. Looking for shelter. Suddenly, they saw it. A huge palace, encrusted with emeralds dancing in the sunlight. Hansel and Gretel immediately had enough courage to knock on the heavy wooden door. They were surprised when a king answered it. 'Please,' they begged, 'could you spare a little food? We're hungry, thirsty and tired.'

'Come in,' declared the king. 'Feel free to have a nap whilst my cooks prepare you a feast to help quench your thirst and satisfy your hunger. You may stay here as long as you wish.'

'Where can we sleep?'

'In the dungeons!'

NADIA HUSSAIN (12)
Old Palace of John Whitgift School, Croydon

I HOPE YOU DON'T MIND BEING ME...

Waiting, waiting for death. How can I escape this wretched tower? If I don't die first, my hair will suffocate me... That's it! My hair!

The prince climbed up a tower, clasping some gorgeous hair for balance. Why? He had heard a rumour of a breathtaking maiden living up there.

Before the poor prince could glimpse at her face, he was knocked unconscious and dragged into the tiny tower room. Rapunzel poured her filthy brew over them both; time seemed to halt for a while. The dagger plunged in and Rapunzel left the tower smirking, 'You don't mind, do you?'

SHREYA PATEL (12)
Old Palace of John Whitgift School, Croydon

JANE EYRE: THE REVENGE

She dreamed. She dreamed of the horrors of her childhood until now. Cruelty from her aunt and cousins. Oh the pains, the punishments, physically and emotionally! Lowood School, where she had friends, but she was often severely punished. Poor Jane didn't do anything. She used to wear a 'Liar' label and stood on a stool. Jane dreamed of Mr Rochester, her love. Rochester's wife, Bertha, was jealous of her. Rochester was killed by the fire at Thornfield Hall. She wanted revenge. Bertha started the fire. Who cared? She was a governess. Bertha had been the cause of her miserable life...

SHANJANA KODEESWARAN (12)
Old Palace of John Whitgift School, Croydon

THE EYES OF THE UNDERWORLD

Down in the Underworld, the three-headed Cerberus was keeping guard. Theseus was approaching. He'd got past the gargantuan gates, next was the canine. Its drool splattered onto the percussive floor. It was asleep. It snored heavily. Theseus went on tiptoe. Silent. He went by almost unnoticed, apart from the dog on the far side. The door was there, black and statuesque. Next thing he was face-to-face with it. Locked. He rattled the handle. He heard a 'Shh.' Startled, he turned to find three giant dog heads growling down at him. Their eyes met, but not for long...

OLIVIA O'SULLIVAN (12)
Old Palace of John Whitgift School, Croydon

THE BOY OF 1818

A girl was walking when she heard a cry. It was a cry that sounded like a child. She was in a haunted house. The cry was from the ghost of a boy who died in 1818. The boy crept up behind the girl. Whoever entered the house never returned back home.
The boy got closer, he was so close to the girl. His plan was to kill her. She was going to have a brutal death just like his. However, the girl turned around and... what happened next, no one knows!

ANUSHKA PATEL (12)
Old Palace of John Whitgift School, Croydon

THE SHATTERED SLIPPER

I was running down the marble steps when suddenly, my glass slipper shattered into pieces. Then my foot started to get really cold and I realised that I was freezing. I was thinking fast, but there was nothing I could do, I would die in complete sadness. Then suddenly, I turned into a big fiery dragon which had not woken up for thousands of years. I stormed back into the ballroom and smashed everything with my bare claw. I looked down. A small figure was waving at me, then kissed me. I was normal. I then stabbed him!

ANIA BASCOMBE (11)
Old Palace of John Whitgift School, Croydon

Lost

My name is Ellie. I'm in a dark, dark place. Lost, all alone and desperate. Will I ever get home? I don't know where I am. I'm clueless as to how Mum and I were separated. I need to find my own way back. I follow this faint greyish path. This seems familiar. I see our car parked in the drive. I've made it home.

I rush through the door, leap onto my Mum's lap and lick her face with my tail wagging with excitement and relief, whilst I promising myself never to leave my lead again!

MYAH SINGH (11)
Old Palace of John Whitgift School, Croydon

Opposite Disgust

Hansel was a quiet boy with wild black hair and tanned skin; unlike Gretel, with her loud voice with slick blonde pigtails.

One afternoon, their mother left them in the woods. Gretel made a frustrated racket, how could a mother leave her children in the woods? Hansel, getting bored of his sister's tantrum, spotted an old wrecked house. He decided he'd go look in it. When Hansel opened the door, he saw delicious, colourful candy walls. Gretel who'd run up shouting at him, paused. She'd witnessed the most disgusting sight, their mother stuffing her face with candy from the walls.

ALICIA OBI (12)
Old Palace of John Whitgift School, Croydon

THE CUPBOARD

I have just moved into a new house in the country. We are now playing hide-and-seek in our new house. There is only one place we're not allowed in - 'The Forbidden Room'. I'm struggling for a place to hide. There is only one place left, 'The Forbidden Room'. I run into the cupboard and I wait. I slowly realise there is no wall at the back! I walk in, it's snowing! I see a strange creature, it's a cross between a cat and a chicken. 'Hello Zaynah,' it says. It knows my name...

ZAYNAH HAFEEZ (12)
Old Palace of John Whitgift School, Croydon

THE CLIFFHANGER

'Twas a sunny morning. I decided to do the outdoor climbing wall for the thousandth time. My friend John moaned, 'Come on Harry, you're always climbing these walls. Let's go to the beach!' I was climbing to practise for a sponsored climb later today. I was harnessed up, halfway up the cliff when my rope snapped! I could go up or down. It would be too steep going up. I decided to give up and come down, then the footing beneath me crumbled away! I had no choice now but to test my strength and willpower and go up...

VICTORIA PERRY (12)
Old Palace of John Whitgift School, Croydon

79

The Three Hungry Pigs

No matter how many times the wolf had tried to get to the pigs, they just wouldn't let him in. He needed another plan. A cunning plan. So he decided that the only way in was by the chimney. That was his biggest mistake. Instead of landing on the warm fireplace as he had expected, he landed in a big saucepan full of boiling water. He had no idea why this saucepan was there, but he soon realised after the three evil pigs placed a lid over him. It was all over... Pigs aren't as cute as they look!

MATHUMITHA BALAKUMARAN (11)
Old Palace of John Whitgift School, Croydon

Granny Kills The Wolf

I got to Granny's front door. I looked through her kitchen window. She sat on top of the wolf, holding a knife by its neck. I silently opened the door. She growled at him, 'Say another word and you're dead.' He shuddered, 'Sorry.' I'm thinking, *why did he speak?* In a flash he was dead.
The very next day I thought, *he didn't deserve to die.* With my magic powder I brought him back to life. Now I regret it to this day because he knocked down the three little pigs' houses. The pigs were eaten before my very eyes.

OLIVIA ROBERTS-ADAMSON (11)
Old Palace of John Whitgift School, Croydon

THE FLAXEN ROPE

His breath edged out from his lips and pressed against the brick. He surveyed the vista of trees that overlooked the village, but returned his eyes to the daunting tower above him. Her hair swung down from the stronghold's edge, and caressed each slab as it returned to the ground, he clasped against its strands. The journey was perturbed with anticipation as he scrutinised each crevice of stone. He lunged for the edge and hauled upwards. His fingers brushed against the marble crescent of the window frame, itching for support. He entered cautiously and turned. She hung; gaunt, pale, deceased.

ANNABELL CLAIRE AGATE (14)
Oriel High School, Crawley

BLOOD PIT

Blood. Filling my mouth, killing me. Blood, from everyone I've ever met, ever known and ever loved. Why? Because I'm a sinner, an outcast, an exile. Left to burn in the blood of every friend I've got and the flesh of fellow sinners. This is my life now. I used to be happy, when I had parents, friends, a home. I gave my blood to the pit with no thought or question. Was I innocent or just blind? At least now I'll die like my parents. Drowned in blood. This is goodbye...

KATIE SEXTON (15)
Oriel High School, Crawley

RESCUED...

Icy liquid rushes onto my throbbing face, creating a sensation of numbness all around. Plunging into my dehydrated mouth. I experience relief from my taste buds that try to savour every unrefined droplet they can. In defiance of my body's every instinct to force my lips shut, in order for me not to live through the never-ending saltiness which continuously floods into my mouth! Suddenly, with an abrupt jolt, my body is thrust against miniscule particles of roughness. Death rejected me once again, he said I was still not ready to leave this life behind, but I knew I was...

YASMIN NOOR
Oriel High School, Crawley

THE WITCH IN THE WOODS

They're here. Their greedy fists smack against my gingerbread walls. They crack sugar sticks from my door, snatch at my furnishings. Coming closer. Getting louder. I hear the crunching of my home in their selfish little gobs. They stomp nearer. There's a bang. They've found it. I walk forwards. It's getting hotter. I reach in front of me, find their spines and press them forward. The brats screech. I hear the sizzling as they burn. I have dinner.

KATIE WEBB (15)
Oriel High School, Crawley

A Genie's Awakening

Stuffed inside a small room, never-ending boredom. The man hadn't seen the light of day in eternity. His mind grew old and didn't have the same shine it used to have. He lay in a scrapyard under layers of rubbish when a boy came scampering over the waste and started to dig. He came across a sequestered lamp. He rubbed the lamp and removed layers of grime. Suddenly, the man awoke, his mind felt clearer than ever before. The man could think faster, he felt better. In happiness, he offered three wishes to the boy, Aladdin.

Ben Furner (12)
Reed's School, Cobham

The Hood

It was a grey, gloomy day and everyone was getting their daily shopping from the market. Suddenly, the market went silent. She had returned. A swell of mutterings slowly filtered through the air.
'I heard the beast killed her grandma.'
'I heard she killed the beast.'
Nobody could see her face; it was covered by her cloak. She had an axe in her hand and a basket in the other. No one had seen her since she left on that fateful day with that same wicker basket. Then, her hood flew off. The truth was revealed. The crowd gasped.

Cameron Smith (12)
Reed's School, Cobham

The Archer

Hansel and I were sprinting through the woods, running for our lives. I could hear pounding footsteps behind me. Suddenly, Hansel fell to the ground like a falling tree, blood spilling out of his back. But then, I was hit, my mouth full of mud, I shrieked. I couldn't move, my legs were bound together. The archer approached me, but of course, he didn't see Hansel wasn't dead! Hansel sneaked up on the archer and with one blow to the head, the archer was surely dead. Wasn't he?

CONNOR HOUSTON (13)
Reed's School, Cobham

Too Much Porridge

Rows of trees. Rows upon rows of trees. Amongst the dark thicket of foliage was a scared, very scared, girl. Her golden locks flowing behind her mixed with mud, twigs and leaves. She ran; not in any particular direction just in a frantic, hurried panic. She looked back. There was nothing there, had she lost them? She stopped and stood still, panting after running so far. A brown flash of fur to her left. A brown flash to her right. She froze. Big blasts of hot air hitting her neck. Behind her was a bear, a hungry bear...

BENJI SEALY (12)
Reed's School, Cobham

GOLDILOCKS

Her stomach grumbled as she craved for some breakfast. 'Mmmmm!' she said as the most pleasant smell flew past her nostrils. She searched, fervently looking side to side. Then, there it was, a crooked old cottage. She slyly crept in and, to her satisfaction, lay the most succulent selection of freshly made porridge. Like a wildebeest, she recklessly munched it up. So full up, she walked to the sofa and lay there elegantly.

'*Roar!*' the bear blurted so viciously. 'Who has been eating my porridge?'

She jumped off the sofa and ran away like a headless chicken!

DARIUS AROUNA (12)
Reed's School, Cobham

HUNTING

There is a piercing grumble of the tall walls, an opening appears. The walls tower over me like an ancient fortress. Then I catch the scent. As I run, hearing their shrieks, I spot them. Sweat drenches their pathetic bodies, fear covers their faces. I see one sprint into the darkness. Then I see one being tugged up into the overgrowth. Then the last one, I know him, somehow. It feels as if he has been drilled into my mind. Trying to escape, he tears through great long vines through the maze. Only one word comes to mind, Tom...

ALEX AHMAD (13)
Reed's School, Cobham

THE WOLF AND THE THREE LITTLE PIGS

The little wolf was grieving over the loss of his dad to a little girl in a red cape. He was starving so he went to the new neighbours, the three pigs, they looked delicious. He knew one was an intelligent pig and would stick up for his brothers. The wolf was stealthy and ate two pigs in one bite. The wolf hunted for the intelligent pig. When he entered the brick house, he noticed a trap and glowing from the basement. So, he sprinted down and without thinking, he ate up the intelligent pig.

CHARLIE LINEHAN (13)
Reed's School, Cobham

THE ESCAPE

I had grown to despise the old woman. It was her that had imprisoned us in these putrid cages and it was her who desired to feast on us. It had been months since we had seen real light and it had been years since we had last seen our father. The old woman unsteadily rose from her rocking chair. She wobbled towards Gretel's cage and unlocked it. Gretel gave out a huge shriek as she struggled in the woman's iron grip. I barged free of my cage and charged forward, sending the woman stumbling into the scorching hot oven.

ZAC SVAROVSKY (13)
Reed's School, Cobham

BEAUTY AND THE BEAST

Frightened for his life, the father was forced to surrender his daughter to the bachelor that was once his host. This daughter was definitely the most caring of them all.
Stumbling into the ballroom, she was petrified to see the beast. His size was daunting, yet she was drawn to his gothic features. Gingerly, she reached out her hand to greet him. His palm felt coarse. Like a swan, they glided gracefully through the vast, derelict ballroom. Enchanted, the beauty was lured into the boundless world of the beast's torment. Bound by fear, the beauty belonged to the beast.

PAUL BROWN-BAMPOE (12)
Reed's School, Cobham

THE TREE

It was dark and had a strange ghostly presence surrounding it. Its hands protruding in odd places with twisted, entangled fingers and its feet coiled into the ground. It wore a rope ring around its dying arm and a man hung from it. Its gnarly skin made me realise just how old it was and its dark hair blocked out the little sun that still remained in the barren sky. It was short, with no transition from its hip to its bare head. But then another presence, not from the tree but somewhere else. The big bad wolf was there...

HARRY HAYLEY (13)
Reed's School, Cobham

THE LION

He caught a glimpse of the lion's fluffy tail. He pursued it silently with a strong grasp on his wooden club. Then he struck the beast's head and wrapped his arm around its neck. Its mane was silky, its eyes were massive and it had bulging muscles in its thighs. It struggled and struggled, but it could not get out of his rock-hard grip. It clawed at his hand but it was no use. It stopped struggling and it went limp. It was dead. He went back to the village and showed the king what he had done.

ALEX PITTARAS (13)
Reed's School, Cobham

PROTECTOR

The mountain lion crept along the weak branch of the tree, stalking the young girl below, waiting for the right time to pounce. The quarter horse reared up and galloped off, leaving the girl alone. Vulnerable. The lion started to purr in excitement of catching his prey. Total silence, no wind, nothing. A twig snapped. The lion turned to the source of the sound. A mustang. Thunder rumbled from the mountains and rain poured as the mustang sprang forward to attack the lion, giving the girl, who sat and watched in awe, a chance to run from imminent danger.

REBECCA ALICE HEALD (13)
Reigate Grammar School, Reigate

GOLDICHOPS

The air was ice-cold as Goldilocks sneaked silently into the house of the three bears. After three loud gunshots, three bears lay dead. She lined them up on their oak table. One was too fat, one was not fat enough but in the middle lay one that was just right. She then cut the bear into a thousand little pieces and she ate every single one. She then leapt up with her mouth covered in the blood of the once savage bear which she had eaten without a single thought. Well, I guess not all stories are nice.

BEN ANDREWS (13)
Reigate Grammar School, Reigate

SWEET HATRED

The girl lay stiff, ghostly, almost dead. Black hair, red lips, skin as white as snow. One kiss would save her. The prince knew this as he gazed softly at her. But such extreme beauty would distract all from his mother. Blood is thicker than water. Raising his sword above his head, the prince stabbed the girl with vile precision. She was gone without a scream. He glared at his missed opportunity, his destroyed destiny. Then, demonically, he grinned.

ELEANOR BRAHAM (14)
Reigate Grammar School, Reigate

THE REAL WEREWOLF

Ragged breath cascades down his thin frame. Bloodshot eyes pierce mine; pleading with me. But I have to see... if he changes. Werewolves are killers. Pa is watching me, testing me. This gruesome shape shifter has to die and I have to kill him.
My heart thrashes as I prepare the changing liquid. Breathe. In one swift movement I pour it over him. But I'm not careful enough. Bristled fur, dagger claws and bloodthirsty fangs shield my vision. A werewolf. It only takes an instant to realise these aren't the boy's features... they are mine.

ANNABELLE PROSSER (13)
Reigate Grammar School, Reigate

NOT A NORMAL HAIRYTALE ENDING

In a country that never rains, a storm was brewing. Her long, straggly hair held her victim in a rat's tail noose. The herd below gazed at the terrified woman edging towards the rim of a window sill eighty feet high. No one expected a scream so loud as her legs became lifeless. There were gasps of horror as the princess hung limply tied up in her own hair. 'Long live Rapunzel!' a single voice murmured as a singular raindrop fell silently.

MILLIE MOORE (14)
Reigate Grammar School, Reigate

Bricked Windows

Three brothers. Pigs. Parted ways to their own accommodation. Lurking. Hunting. A beast. Feared by all. A wolf. He sensed his chance. A delicious dinner. One almighty blow. The fragile straw structure collapsed. The pig took refuge in his brother's mud house. The wolf, having not eaten in hours, chased the pig and reached the house. Another blow. Knockout. The pigs sprinted to their elder brother's house. They screamed and shouted for him to open the door. However, as a new law stated you had to pay tax for windows, the elder brother had bricked them up. Dinner was served.

OLLY KAIL (13)
Reigate Grammar School, Reigate

You're A Fool If You Fall

He heard a voice, like silk. Entrancing. He saw the tower, no doors. Inviting? A window! It drew him in like a mosquito to a light. A rope? No. Hair! He climbed anyway. Why be scared? He entered uninvited. An aura around her, glowing red, he could not tear his eyes away. Once his met hers, those soulless caverns, he knew this was a mistake. He tried to run with all his might. It was no use. 'You're not going anywhere,' the siren sneered, a hole appeared below him. 'You're mine now.' He fell. Nobody leaves that tower!

JEMIMA WILLIAMS (14)
Reigate Grammar School, Reigate

91

DARK SNOW

A beautiful young girl, with innocent eyes, people didn't know that this was a disguise. She was an evil genius who took the lives of everyone she met. She had been banished to the meadow surrounding the kingdom where these innocent seven dwarfs interrupted her singing. They asked her if she was lost and if she needed a place to stay. So she thought to herself, *my next victim I think*.

CARYS EDWARDS (13)
Reigate Grammar School, Reigate

THE MAN WITH A FACE OF DEATH

The train crash had killed 100 men and women. They'd closed off the railway and the building it collided with. I was one for adventure, so in the dead of night I left to look for him: the only survivor whose face was so mangled he hid in the building. I climbed the catwalk to the old sleeping quarters. A rush of anger, a scream of death. I fell from 50 floors up...
While the paramedic checked my vitals, I looked up. There he was, the man with a face of death. He wasn't a man, he was Death.

JAMIE HOLLOWAY (14)
Reigate Grammar School, Reigate

Flight 94

He had 50 seconds. He was the only one who could help. As thick red blood trickled under the battered door, Billy was out of options. He looked around for ideas, a shard of glass, a broken arm rest, all can be used. Billy approached the cockpit, with a glass shard in one hand, heart beating. The plane jolted. The door opened ajar. Billy's hand raised, he opened the door. *Bang!*

Benjamin Hudson (13)
Reigate Grammar School, Reigate

Tears

The lights flickered off. The luminous black darkness shone bright. A heavy breath blew against the woman's neck. *Drip.* She was still. A man's lips reached for hers. *Drip.* She was still. The silence in the room screamed loud; loud until he drew up a knife. *Drip.* Gradually the sound of someone neatly sawing wood grew louder, grew faster. The door opened, beaming a bright light onto the man. Cutting the rope which was tied around her neck. 'I'm sorry,' he whispered gently, whilst lowering her still body to the ground. *Drip,* as another sorry tear dripped down his face.

Lara Bertin (14)
Reigate Grammar School, Reigate

SAVAGE SILENCE

There was a blinding flash of white light. This was it. These were the final days of our crippled race. A lab-contained virus had mutated out of control and infected millions. Days later, all of New York was infected with the putrid virus. However I don't like to dwell on the past, it's too late for that. My friend John and I were the only known survivors of this savage plague. *Boom!* There goes the sun. It's been forming into a supernova lately. Oh well, as my father used to say, it's good to go out with a bang.

SEBASTIAN SAVAGE (13)
Reigate Grammar School, Reigate

ONE OF THEM

Cool breezes brushed briskly off Daisy's shoulder. The morning was hot as she strolled on, the ground already baking, heat haze visible everywhere she looked. A dizzy spell dawned upon her and a rush of blood ascended to her head. The cold, wrinkly hands sprawled over her getting a grip... She was whisked wildly away. She noticed as the light grew brighter in her eyes, the numbing sensation of rainwater dripping off the corpse-like figure. An overpowering force overcame her as a brittle bony finger touched her, she was one of them now...

WILL POORT (14)
Reigate Grammar School, Reigate

ONLY ONE LEFT!

Knock, knock. He was there. *Huff, puff.* The straw wouldn't hold. *Crash!* The house was down, the race had started. First one to Piggy Twigs! Piggy Straw won, but it wasn't over! *Huff, puff.* The twigs tumbled down. Phase two began! To Piggy Bricks' house! They turned back to look for the wolf, he wasn't there. But they sprinted on. The door was already open. The wolf's lifeless body lay on the floor, rope burns all over him and a red bullet hole in his head. Piggy Bricks turned, *bang, bang!*
'They were no good either!' he said.

ELIZABETH HANLON (13)
Reigate Grammar School, Reigate

CINDERELLA

She ran from the ball, tears flooding down her face; she knew she had to go. She stumbled down the steps, managing to lose a shoe. Nevertheless she ran, and ran into the woods; 'Cinderella, Cinderella,' he called. She kept going, until she was alone. Well, she wasn't completely alone; something else was after her too. She stood still, breathing heavily. Branches cracked as it grew nearer. It snarled and growled. She screamed, backing away from the beast. Slowly, it came towards her. Both she and the beast knew she was doomed. She wished she had stayed.

STEPH WEBER (14)
Reigate Grammar School, Reigate

The True Tale Of The Titanic

The slow humming of the coal engines used to turn the massive blades of the propeller. It was a peaceful evening, the stars were out, the cold air of the Arctic was still. Suddenly, he was thrown from his feet, the ship lurched, then... Darkness fell upon the ship with only the moonlight for guidance. Then it grabbed the funnel. Explosions started and screams... Ceased. The huge tentacles picked him up and plunged him under along with others and the ship! He saw the hull sinking alongside him. Darkness grew as it wrapped around, the drowning screams were never heard.

Jack Watkins (13)
Reigate Grammar School, Reigate

Why She's That Way

'Are you OK?'
'Yeah, I'm OK.' She looks alright with her calm brown eyes... She slightly ascends her chin and arrows her eyes towards me. The first thing I can't help but notice are her eyes - they're not brown anymore - they've turned a demonic pale grey and have pupils like a snake's. At once, I freeze, not expecting that change. 'I was OK before, now I'm great - feeling great to slide these nails and tear you to bloody shards.' I stand paralysed, unable to react - I yelp in shock - she hasn't failed to blade my insides far too deep.

Puja Madhyanum (14)
Reigate Grammar School, Reigate

CONDEMNED

Magic. It had doomed him, he knew, as Camelot's fine knights advanced upon him. Rage burned inside him like a witch's potion, as the nearest knight drew his sword from its sheath. His family were gone and he wished that he too were slain by the mighty king, Uther Pendragon. Tears pricked his eyes like a gentle touch of needles. With the cunning of a fox, he raised his open hand and clenched it into a fist of fury that burned like venom. The knights fell backwards.

LILY GOLD (14)
Reigate Grammar School, Reigate

AN UNFORTUNATE EVENT

In the dark forest, a young girl named Goldilocks came across a red brick house. She knocked but there was no answer. She then cautiously opened the door and the house was empty, or so she thought. The smell of warm porridge drew her closer to where three beasts were eating. With a loud roar, a beast shouted, 'Who goes there?' With a scream Goldilocks sprinted back to the door, but the lumbering hairy beast got there first. She acted quickly, ran up the stairs and saw a window. She jumped out and with a hollow thud, everything went black.

TOM BUSHELL (14)
Reigate Grammar School, Reigate

THE AXE MAN

Screech! Screech! was the only sound made by the axe man as he sat there on a tree trunk, a cap on his head and two women at his feet. A wolf sat on its hind legs next to him. He raised his sharpened axe high and brought it down swiftly. An almighty thud was heard as screams surrounded him. The wolf, deciding the man was done, pounced on the girl with a red cloak and an old woman with grey hair and stiff limbs. The man, meanwhile, raised his axe high once more and his axe tasted of blood.

MAX WALKER LONG (14)
Reigate Grammar School, Reigate

THE DISGUISE

I must get rid of them, before they wreck my marriage. They hate their stepmother. I don't know why. She does everything for them. They are such spoilt, jealous kids. They bleed me dry and steal sweets from the dear old lady's sweet shop on the edge of the forest. Off they run, innocently plotting to thieve her stack of sweets in the back of the shop. They'd never suspect I was disguised as the old lady.
They they were, raiding her store as I crept up behind them and shoved them in the roaring flames. My vile children, dead.

LUCY MARTIN (13)
Reigate Grammar School, Reigate

TWISTED RED RIDING HOOD

Little Red Riding Hood was walking to her grandma's little cottage in the dark, eerie woods when suddenly she saw a humongous, intimidating wolf charging at her. She screamed, she started to panic. Then, out of nowhere, appeared a tall, young man holding a rifle. He took the black rifle and, just before the wolf leapt up to bite Red Riding Hood, he shot it, but he missed. The wolf was still alive but Red Riding Hood had been shot. There on the floor lay Red Riding Hood, blood seeping out of her head. The young man now a murderer.

SERINA CLIFF-PATEL (14)
Reigate Grammar School, Reigate

THE GOLDEN FLEECE

The metal door slams. Every evening, like cruel clockwork, she would come. Pointing her sharp tiny scissors at my face. Abusing my vulnerability as she starts to snip. The sound alone makes me shudder, and thorny fingernails jab my back in disdain. Every day she steals a little extra until I am nothing more than a bare, cracked scalp. As she swoops out of the room, seizing today's haul, I scout the grimy floor and clasp the forsaken snippets. My lavish gold has been ripped from me. As if I was a sheep. Perhaps, to them, I am.

SOPHIE JOSEPHINE HARDING (14)
Reigate Grammar School, Reigate

99

THE BEAST WHO CRIED WOLF

He howled at night. The villagers came to slay the beast, torches ablaze, only to find a boy, lying amongst the leaves of the gloomy forest. They cursed him and returned to their homes. Each night he howled, each night they came and each night the belief of the supernatural killer diminished. Until, the next full moon, he called but nobody came. His pleas grew bigger, even the moon could hear, but still nobody came. As a dark cloud hid the glistening moon, orange eyes transformed green. All that remained was a beast who cried wolf.

KHUSHVEER DHILLON (14)
Reigate Grammar School, Reigate

RAPUNZEL, UNCOVERED

'Rapunzel, Rapunzel, let down your hair.' The hair came down and up she went. 'I've got our next target lined up - looks like we'll be eating tonight!' she cackled.
'I call the heart,' Rapunzel croaked; sharpening her knife in the dark corner of the room. Stepping into the light she gave her mother a fright, she never took off her wig to show her blood-red hair. 'His name?'
'Prince Arthur of Camelot... '
'Rapunzel, Rapunzel let down your hair, I've come for you, please let me in,' the prince called up the tower.
'Quick, put on your disguise... '

NIKI OVERTOOM (13)
Reigate Grammar School, Reigate

ALICE'S NOT SO WONDERFUL WONDERLAND

I dozed off. Down, down, down the rabbit hole I fell, clocks and keys fell beside me. The Queen of Hearts with her extravagant dress and crazy hair stood in front of me, holding the eight of clubs' head, blood dripping onto the black and white chequered floor. She screamed 'Pastry!' The little white rabbit ran to her. She squeezed the head to fill her jam tarts - 'Ready for sale!' she shouted.

I suddenly awoke from my strange repetitive 'Wonderland' dream. My straight jacket too tight. You see, society struggles to understand the insane. We 'make up stories' apparently.

MEGAN FINCH (14)
Reigate Grammar School, Reigate

GREED. ENVY. CRUELTY

Beauty surrounded her. She wasn't out of place at the party. Her long, flowing dress and shimmering silver shoes. But there was an ominous shadow cast over her. The shadow of envy and jealousy cast by her sisters. They were jealous of her carriage, her stallions, her hair and her spouse. For he was the most noble prince in all of New York. He was rich, handsome, clever, humorous. Every girl's dream. He was happy, she was happy. But the sisters? The sisters only knew greed. The sisters only knew jealousy and envy. The sisters only knew pain and cruelty...

SAM ARCHER (14)
Reigate Grammar School, Reigate

THE WOMAN NEXT DOOR

They had to leave us there. They had nothing. We should have never gone with Maureen though, I could see the intention in her eyes. I knew she would try what she did, with the amount of years with abusive adults, we can see it from a mile off. The cottage seemed so subtle, joined on with the room, the cooking room. It was that night, she leapt for Gretel, my sister. It was complete self-defence, I grabbed the thing nearest to me. It happened to be a kitchen knife. I did not kill her, the knife did.

JARRETT MEE (13)
Reigate Grammar School, Reigate

MY JOURNEY TO NEW BEGINNINGS

His face holds the same smile I had always known, but it was no longer gentle and comforting. The last time I saw the wolf, we did not speak, we walked closer, his eyes glinting in the sunlight. I drew my knife, inspected the blade and saw it staring back at me. This was my chance to start my life afresh. I took my shot, right in the heart, the blood gushing from his chest, that was it. I was never to see that wolf again, and never did... I had to return to the asylum!

GENEVIEVE COLLIER (13)
Reigate Grammar School, Reigate

THE WITCH

The witch breathed the air. Young. The undergrowth rustled. They were coming closer. Waiting. She braced herself. *Almost there,* she thought. Just a little closer. The scent was stronger. There were two? Tonight's meal would be a fine one! She licked her lips. The meal was near. She could hear the footsteps. Two squirrels, babies, scurried past. Sigh. She turned to re-enter her house. 'Please madam, might we have some bread?' a girl's voice uttered. The old woman smiled maliciously with intense satisfaction.

MAX GOLDBLOOM (14)
Reigate Grammar School, Reigate

THE SIREN IN THE TOWER

The bewitched rider ploughed on, following the enchanting voice to a tower which appeared through the flora. The voice echoed from the tower and as he reached the base he saw blonde hair cascading down the side. Still entranced, he started to ascend the locks. The higher he got, the more his mind cleared. As he watched, the ground crumbled into an abyss. A window appeared, through which a girl was visible. She lay rigid, singing and that was when he heard another voice. 'You won't wake her, she will see you in Hell!' Then the tresses he gripped vanished...

MEGAN THURGOOD (13)
Reigate Grammar School, Reigate

Never-Ending

The flames grew as the wood burnt, taking the danger with it. Innocent and sweet, cursed close to birth, she didn't have a choice. Only a prick in a needle would send her to sleep. It happened. Years passed and she didn't wake. As still as a statue, her pale face didn't have life anymore, not a twinkle in her eye. All the people had no life, also still. She wasn't dead, no, just sleeping, dreaming, the prick on her finger going round in her head. He kissed her rosy red lips, nothing happened. She wasn't going to wake again!

Sophie Nathan
Reigate Grammar School, Reigate

Hatred Forgotten

A young teenager of German origin was roaming the streets of London. He stumbled along drunk and fell into a deep sleep. An Englishman saw him, he took him into his house and cared for him. He taught him how to play the beautiful game. He was passed from academy to academy, but never settled down. Always saying, 'My dad was my greatest coach.' He was approached to go to a German trial. He said, 'If I make it to national level, I will play for England because the greatest man I've met is English.' He made it.

Tom Allen (13)
Reigate Grammar School, Reigate

THE THIEF

Slumber had reached out its greedy hands and stolen everything from the child that lay on the bed, never stirring. Her beauty had gone, the pure angelic look on her face vanished and replaced by a haggard, weary appearance. No longer a princess sleeping, now a corpse long dead. After climbing brambles, branches and briars, at the end of his long search, the prince arrived ready to wake his sleeping beauty, still innocent from her 100 years' rest. But she wasn't his serene princess anymore. A true love's kiss would be no good now, it would not work on her.

FREYA SHAYLOR (13)
Reigate Grammar School, Reigate

RAPUNZEL

A prince! A real prince has come to save me! Rapunzel thought as she let down her hair.
'I'm coming to save you,' he said, tugging on her hair. Immediately she noticed how much heavier he was and held onto each side of the window for support. The prince struggled to lift himself up, for everything was done for him in the castle. Her arms started shaking from the strain, she couldn't hold on for much longer. He slipped and fell, then grabbed back on, but the weight was too much, and Rapunzel fell out the window, onto the ground!

JAMES SHIPLEY (13)
Reigate Grammar School, Reigate

The Princess And The Monster

The princess went to bed. She slept. She woke up in the night. She could feel something digging into her mattress. She got up, lit her torch and looked under the bed. Nothing there... She heard a scuttle across her room. She turned instantly and cursed whatever was there. The princess was terrified and was breathing heavily. She ran to get her father's sword so she could defend herself against whatever was there. She turned to go back to her room, then she suddenly stopped still. She felt a breath on her neck. She turned around and there it stood...

Jonny Bridges (13)
Reigate Grammar School, Reigate

Clive's Stash

Today I found a map with a cross saying, 'Clive's stash'. I went to find this place and it was an old, decrepit, abandoned building filled with junk. Surprisingly, I decided to explore this intriguing place. I saw underneath an old wooden beam, a fantastic, glistening, golden piece. I decided to pull it out from underneath. Suddenly, everything shook and the roof began to fall in on me. I quickly dashed with the heavy gold piece out of the building. I thought I would get stuck there for good, never getting found, but I came out alive, with a memento.

Zohair Farooq (14)
Reigate Grammar School, Reigate

Karma: Not All Wolves Are Bad

Wilf Wolf was collecting for the homeless pigs' charity. At Piggy Straw's flat, no sooner had he reached the door when Piggy Straw huffed and puffed through the letterbox at him. Wilf wandered sadly away.
At Piggy Wood's bungalow, Wilf was met with more huffing and puffing. Tail firmly between his legs, he walked away. A crowd of pigs gathered outside Piggy Brick's mansion. No huffing and puffing there! The pigs charged at Wilf, he ran for his life, dropping the empty collection pot as he fled. Later that day, a freak hurricane hit Piggy Town, destroying all the houses.

Greg Lewis (13)
Reigate Grammar School, Reigate

Being Alone At War

Fear. Worry. War. The worst thing to be in. I just want to be home. I see people die every day. I see my friends die every day. I can never sleep at night. The constant worry of dying. I've been here for so long now. Grenades everywhere around the cold, dark trenches.
I feel isolated, petrified and there's no one there for me anymore. Nightmares every night of the deaths. The blood, the gore, I can see it all. The constant fear that I'll be next. I'm all alone with nothing left.

Ethan May (13)
Reigate Grammar School, Reigate

The Three Boars

Dark red eyes squinting at the ruined shack, their razor-sharp tusks dripping with crimson blood. The ground was disturbed beneath their feet from where the pounding hooves scraped at barren dirt. Ready to charge. All together they dashed towards the hut. Again. Again. Until finally it collapsed in one dusty heap. From underneath the scraps, a rugged, frightened wolf limped out on a barely recognisable leg. A bloody stump of flesh with a white glint of bare bone sticking out. With one glance at the three boars, he let out a terrified yelp and fled into the dark woods.

Jack Wilson-Smith (14)
Reigate Grammar School, Reigate

Huff, Puff, Poof!

His wiry tail whipped the ground, cracking when it struck the concrete. He filled his lungs to bursting point. He would eat those pigs tonight. He would sure have a feast tonight. However, the pigs had others ideas, they were not going down with their house. The beast pulled the plug. Cold air hit the house like a herd of rhinoceros ploughing into the brick walls. Cement was torn from between the bricks. The house crumbled as the beast finished shooting air towards his dinner. He looked up with a grin, but saw no little pigs cowering beneath the rubble...

Louis Thomas (13)
Reigate Grammar School, Reigate

THE WRONG HUT

The wolf. The predator. Hunting his prey who survived. The darkness, his friend in barren land. Three pigs were hiding away, scared of night, in the dark. As he ran through the night, the glistening moonlight shimmered off the lake. He howled, had a scent of three animals cowering away. As the wolf kept running, he heard a sad yelp, and a wolf darted back past the assassin, but he kept running. As he cleared the forest, a house made of straw stood grand. He growled and pounced, but out came a man. *Bang!*

HARRY PACKHAM (13)
Reigate Grammar School, Reigate

VIOLENCE OF INSANITY

Zeb shot through the forest, silently screaming in fear from his nightmarish pursuer. As he turned his head, he let out a short, sharp scream as he violently tumbled over a root into a narrow ditch. Echoing his scream was an immense roar that tore through the forest after Zeb, shredding the leaves off the trees. He tried to get up, he tried to run, he tried to get away, but there was no escape for him now. The ogre vehemently erupted through the tree line, coming to a dizzying halt. Roughly sniffing the air, his prey was trapped.

SEVI WEBB (14)
Reigate Grammar School, Reigate

109

THE TRAVELLER AND THE LISTENER

Long ago, there lived a family in a house in the middle of the forest. One day, a traveller came across this house. The family asked him to come back in exactly a year, to help protect them and their house. He made his promise and left!
A year and one day later... He was too late. The man that could have saved them failed. He knocked on the door, but there was no answer. The traveller never found out how the family died. Legend has it that there is still a little boy living there, listening, but never answering...

IMMY WARD (13)
Steyning Grammar School, Steyning

THE PERFECT PRINCE?

Her hair fell down for the last time ever, the breeze was light and the sun was shining. As she galloped off with her handsome prince, her hair swaying behind her, she realised something. She was free, not just from the tower, but from the wicked witch too. Her days of fear were gone and her days of childhood were over. She had met her perfect man. Or had she? She saw a metal structure laying ahead. It looked almost like a cage and they where heading straight for it...

AIMEE SCARLET COLLIS-STEPNEY (13)
Steyning Grammar School, Steyning

THE THREE WOLVES AND THE BIG BAD PIG

Three wolves came to the age of independence. They made their own homes. One made it out of straw, one of sticks and one of bricks. The thing the wolves feared most, was Big Bad Pig. They built their homes and went to bed. Pig had been watching them building. He decided to teach the naive wolves a lesson.

Pig drove his Ferrari into the first house. It collapsed and the wolf ran to his brother. Pig drove into the house of sticks. The two wolves ran to the house of bricks. The car drove into the house of bricks...

JOSEPH O'REILLY (13)
Steyning Grammar School, Steyning

RED RIDING HOOD'S SWEET DISASTER

Here I go again. The same path for the 100th time. I love my grandma.

I pick up the basket and start my mile journey through the depths of the gloomy forest. Halfway there, I see a shadow swoop past the path in front of me, I stop. My heart pounding heavily. 'Hello,' I scream, but no reply. I carry on, but I can't forget what I just saw. Suddenly, it is there. A wolf. I stumble back and I tumble down a hill. There is a house. It's made of sweetness. I step inside. I burn to my death.

GABRIEL REDDING (13)
Steyning Grammar School, Steyning

111

THE MAGIC BEAN

A little boy planted magic beans. He went to sleep that night, excited at the thought of a big bean. He woke up the next morning. He ran outside and looked up at the tall green plant. He started to climb. He got higher and looked down in amazement at the height. He carried on climbing. He got to the top and looked around. Nothing. He carried on looking in awe, but then he saw an old poor man. 'Are you OK?' he asked.
'Help.'
So the boy gave the man some beans so he could sell them for money.

CALLUM RUSSELL (13)
Steyning Grammar School, Steyning

BEASTIE

A shiver ran through my body as I stumbled through the darkness. I could hear the floor creaking as if something was in there. Something was circling me, watching me, lurking among the darkness. What was it?
A sudden movement caught my eye. I took a step, each step taking me deeper and deeper into the room. The silence broke with a clap of lightning. I turned to see a pair of dark blue eyes flaring into mine. It towered above me, but the beast seemed startled, scared. His tail between his legs, he collapsed to the floor, silently whimpering.

LAURYL HANNAH RENCONTRE (14)
Steyning Grammar School, Steyning

CINDERELLA'S TRUE PRINCE

As Cinderella gracefully danced with the prince, he spoke into her ear, 'You are my Queen no matter what you think!' It was this moment Cinderella knew she had to leave straight away from this menacing man, but in her movement, her shoe fell off. 'Get back here now you silly girl!' Cinderella turned back to see the prince's fury-filled eyes. She turned back around and fled out of the castle with her heart thumping and eyes watering. The last words heard as she left the castle were, 'I will find you and you will regret disobeying the prince!'

KIRSTIE SERVANTE (14)
Steyning Grammar School, Steyning

POISON APPLE

Snow White saw the haggard old woman out of the corner of her eye. After months of being beaten, abused and eventually abandoned by her stepmother, she had been wandering the forest for weeks. Surviving on a diet of wild berries and forest creatures, she was a fragment of her former beautiful self, with twigs knotting her hair and scratches tearing her legs; the forest hadn't been kind. As the woman handed the apple to her, they exchanged a final glance. Fully knowing her fate, Snow White bit into the apple as her stepmother stood gleefully over her.

POPPY MALE (13)
Steyning Grammar School, Steyning

Little Red Riding Hood

Once upon a time, there was a girl called Little Red Riding Hood. She lived with her mum and one day left to visit her grandmother in the woods close by. A wolf was present in the forest and was extremely hungry and asked Little Red Riding Hood where she was going. She told the wolf that she was going to visit her grandmother who was not well. Little Red Riding Hood detected the wolf was not good so increased her speed to her grandmother where she found an old axe. When the wolf arrived she cut his head off.

HARRY TEAGUE (14)
Steyning Grammar School, Steyning

Bang!

Bang! Everything went quiet except for my loud footsteps and my heavy breathing. I knew that my head was in his scope. The rusty car lay lifeless on a bed of sand. I hid, scared. Gunfire echoing through the air. I reloaded my gun, ready. I knew where he was, but if I moved, I was in the line of fire. I kicked up a cloud of dust and sand, running for further cover. Boots covered in blood, I took aim. I shot him right between the eyes. Watching him fall to his death, off the gritty balcony. *Bang!*

DAVID KNIGHT (12)
Steyning Grammar School, Steyning

SAW III

Jeff was walking down the dark corridor and there was writing on the door. It said: 'Time for payback!' Jeff walked in the room and the door slammed shut with the other guy that Jeff saved before. Right in front of them was a man. Jeff's face crumpled as he looked at the man. 'It's the guy who killed my son!' The time started and the guy who killed Jeff's son was hooked onto the thing called the wrack! The wrack twisted the guy's arms all the way around until the bones snapped! Jeff didn't try helping!

JACK BRIDLE (13)
Steyning Grammar School, Steyning

RAMBLE? MORE LIKE RAMBO

Running as fast as my legs could carry me, I glanced back to check if he was following me. No, he was nowhere to be seen. 'You really thought I would just leave you alone Jenkins? Well I'm not. It's never as simple as that. It would be a lot harder to get rid of someone such as myself.' He spat in my direction. I guess I wasn't rid of him.
'You know you tend to ramble?'
'Ramble? More like Rambo.' With that he plunged the knife into my chest. Having a psycho brother-in-law isn't that great.

GERTIE CAMERON (12)
Steyning Grammar School, Steyning

Zombocalypse

I was happy, cool, loved, smart, popular, fun, alive... A boy's scream pierced the night as bullets would to glass. I sat up straight in bed, thinking it was a nightmare. I looked out of the window and the boy screamed once more and then stopped with a sickening, choking sound. Suddenly, I was sweating with fear. Pain exploded in my head and then I realised I wasn't alone. I never was. I saw its rotting flesh and bones. This was what killed the boy. A zombie! Then darkness claimed me forever. It was the end.

JACOB EMIN (11)
Steyning Grammar School, Steyning

Falling

Splish, splash, splosh. You may know the story of Jack and Jill, but not everything you were told is true... They did go up the hill, but not to fetch a pail of water. They were under hypnosis; they were being summoned by the crockalist, a creature that feasts on children. *Bang!* Jack fell down the well and hit the bottom. Jill tried to saved him, but fell in too. The crockalist appeared above the well to hear snarling inside... There was more than just one predator in the woods. What devoured Jack and Jill?

ELEANOR CATHERINE KEEGAN (11)
Steyning Grammar School, Steyning

The Actual Story Of The Sphinx

The boy came into view. 'Here we go, a nice meal, a little thin but appetising.' He still approached. When he got close enough, I leapt into action.

I shouted in my commanding voice, 'I am the Sphinx. In order to pass, answer my question: What walks on four legs in the morning, two in the afternoon and three in the evening?'

'A goat?' he replied.

'Wrong, now I'm going to eat you!'

'Wait!' he cried. 'I'll build you a massive statue of you if you eat my sister instead of me!'

'You'd better!' I growled. She was divine.

JESSICA BROWN (12)
Steyning Grammar School, Steyning

Goodbye

'Are you okay?' I ask Tom, rubbing his belly.

'Yeah. I'm just going to the shop to get some food, okay?'

'Okay.'

Boom! Crash! Bang! Then it happened, the day that everything changed.

Beep, beep, the heart monitor blaring in my ear.

'Hold my hand,' Tom gasped as he held out his icy, wintry palm. 'I love you Layla. Goodbye,' he murmured quietly. He coughed. He drew his last breath. *Beep! Boom, boom, boom!* The sound of my aching heart, broken by death, the heart breaker. I place all of our hopes and dreams on Thomas' lifeless body.

ISABELLE DAISY OGDEN (11)
Steyning Grammar School, Steyning

Two Robbers

There were two robbers called Tom and Sam. They were very good friends and they had known each other for a long time.
One day, Sam wanted money to buy his birthday present, but his parents were so poor, so he decided to rob it. Tom helped him as well. They robbed money on the street, school and so on. They felt so excited because they could but lots of things, but, unfortunately, a woman took a photo of them when they were robbing money and she called the police to come. A few minutes later, they were arrested.

MIKI CHUI (14)
Steyning Grammar School, Steyning

Magical

When I enrolled for the sorcerer's school, I was expecting fun. I was expecting magical sorcerer friends, mad, ditzy teachers; maybe some calamitous but ultimately comedic lessons. I expected every day to be an adventure that wrapped itself up neatly and tucked me into bed at night. Well let me tell you something: false advertising. I was not expecting that I'd be kidnapped on the first day. I was also definitely not thinking that I would be stuffed into a dog cage and prepared for satanic sacrifice. Apparently this is a normal thing for first-years. Induction ceremony? Huh, fun.

ABIGAIL EDWARDS (15)
The Eastbourne Academy, Eastbourne

SLEEPING BEAUTY

A curse was put on the young princess, when she turned 16, she would prick her finger and she would go into a deep sleep. For years the king summoned all the spinning wheels to be destroyed. However one day, Sleep Beauty explored the castle, into the darkest dungeons, through the doors, she came across the last spinning wheel. Her finger was pricked and she instantly fell into a sleep... almost like death. The king sent his men to find her as she had been gone for days... No one dared to check the dungeons where Sleeping Beauty still lays.

FEITONG WILDE (13)
The Eastbourne Academy, Eastbourne

RAPUNZEL

The prince wandered through the dense woods, lost. He stopped and gazed back to see shimmering blond locks hanging down from a mossy stone turret. He ran over to the hidden castle and called up to the beautiful princess who was gazing down at him with hope. As he started talking, she quickly cut him off, 'Shhhh, climb my hair and get me down, please.' Love-struck, he quickly started climbing her hair like a rope. As he put his leg on the window sill, his dagger on his belt cut her hair and he fell to his death.

ANYA CHAMPAGNE (13)
The Eastbourne Academy, Eastbourne

Sugar Sweet

She ran. Hot, thick blood gushed from the gash in her side, whilst her brother's agonising screams pounded in her head. Unforgiving cackles tormented her as she crashed through never-ending woods and as she looked back, she saw scarlet-red eyes glaring at her behind the hood of the cloaked figure stalking her. Branches scratched and tore at her face, but she never stopped running. The darkness enclosed her and the figure loomed even closer. A sickly sweet smell hit her as she broke through the trees. Back at the gingerbread house, and back at her doom...

Zoe Smith (13)
The Warwick School, Redhill

Goldilocks And The Three Bears

Once, in a kingdom called Hyrlew, a little girl called Goldilocks was wandering through a forest. Soon she found an old cottage, nicely tidied and clean! She knocked on the door, but no one answered! Being a brat like spoilt Goldilocks was, she simply walked in! She ate their porridge and broke their chairs. Then she went to sleep in their beds! When the owners came home, who were angry, savage bears; they woke up Goldilocks and burned her head with flaming metal poles and ripped her limbs off with single slashes. Later, her mother found her and screamed!

Skye Jennings (12)
The Warwick School, Redhill

CINDERS' DEATH

This was it, her chance to shine. She would go to the ball, but that wasn't what would happen. As Cinders arrived, she realised her mistake. This was no ordinary ball and the prince was no ordinary prince. As she entered the ballroom, it all became crystal clear. The ball was just a front. Bodies were scattered across the floor. Blood smeared over the ornate golden tiles. She was next, she could tell. He walked menacingly towards her. Blood ran down her pale neck as claw-like nails dug into her neck. She'd died before she hit the floor.

AMY BARTLETT (13)
The Warwick School, Redhill

THE APPLE OF DEATH

The apple was as red as the blood that trickled down her face. The figure came closer and closer.
It finally reached her face and whispered in her ear, 'This is the end, give up now or this knife will just get deeper.' The smell of death filled the air as the knife slowly sliced across her neck. She screamed in pain, but she knew it was too late, crimson blood poured from her body, her eyes dropped out and her head rolled across the floor. 'This will teach you not to pick the apple of death.'

BECCA HISCOCKS (13)
The Warwick School, Redhill

REAL WORLD TERROR

'Soon,' said the careers advisor, 'you will become adults, and with that, there will be a whole new set of responsibilities for you to deal with...'
At these terrible words, the class of children shuddered, their hearts filling with icy dread and bile burned the backs of their throats.
'This will include dealing with applying for bank loans for tuition fees, mortgages...'
The children began to shake in fear.
'And finally, you will have to apply for university...'
The class was thrown into turmoil. I think someone threw up. The future seemed increasingly crap. Why were they bothering again?

BEULAH BERRISFORD
The Warwick School, Redhill

THE HEADLESS HORSE INN

In a village a long time ago, there was a famous horse rider. The horse rider's horse was named Lightning because the horse was fast. One night, while in the stable, Lightning was attacked by a gang of kidnappers. A nearby police officer was watching and chased them. Terrified, the kidnappers cut the horse's head off instead of the rope holding him and ran off. They built an inn named the Headless Horse to remember Lightning. Some say in the middle of the night, the headless horse can be seen still searching for its lost head.

JAMIE FENSOM
The Warwick School, Redhill

122

SLEEPING FOREVER

It's my 16th birthday today and I've been woken up at 7:00 to fetch some berries. I think, *it's my day to relax, not a day full of chores*. So I wander through the forest and meet this handsome young man. We dance through the morning before I realise I still haven't got any berries. I invite the stranger back, but before, we must pick some berries. They look ripe and tasty although I got told to only pick certain ones. Oh no! I forgot what colour. This could be the end. I try one and...

REBECCA McDONOUGH (12)
Therfield School, Leatherhead

RUN, LITTLE RED RIDING HOOD, RUN

Red meandered between the throng of soaring pine trees and a small girl - fragile and pale, with wisps of blonde hair across her face; panting and running, running for the sake of life. She had met a huntsman who had warned her of the beast that roamed the forest and panicked for her grandmother who lived in the same forest. Finally arriving, she knocked upon the heavy oak door, hoping and praying that her grandmother was okay. Her grandmother called for her to enter. Sitting down, she wiped her forehead and looked at her grandmother... wait, who?

SHEREE-RANIA USMAN BINASING (14)
Therfield School, Leatherhead

THE TOWER AND THE WOLF

The princess climbed down the tower, she had to get away. Quickly, she ran as fast as she could away from the tower, her keeper, her life that she knew. Rapunzel's long blonde hair kept getting caught around tree trunks, she kept running. All of a sudden, she heard a rustling, but thought nothing of it and kept running. Before she knew it, a wolf came and attacked her. She wasn't scared though, she didn't care. Rapunzel just let the wolf attack her. The wolf only wanted her hair though. Why? Why does he want her hair? She didn't care.

DANIELLE CUNNINGTON (14)
Therfield School, Leatherhead

GRUMPY'S REVENGE

Many months have passed since Snow White spoke her gentle, calming voice. She lays still. Peaceful yet daunting. That apple really took a turn for the worst. Every passing week I remove a fingernail from my own much loved miner's hands. I feel that I must inflict pain to myself as a punishment for not being there for the woman I love. That wretched prince thinks he can steal her from me. I'll show him. When the time is right, I shall cut him at the stomach and pull his skin up over his head. Suffocating him in his skin.

MATT WILKINS (14)
West Sussex Alternative Provision College, Burgess Hill

THE STORY OF HOW HEROBRINE BECAME EVIL – A MINECRAFT TALE

One day while Notch and Herobrine were mining, they came across an enormous ravine filled with shining diamonds. They could be rich! Day and night was spent mining and battling countless zombies and skeletons with their iron armour and swords. Yet when they were nearly done, a pesky enderman came to battle. He was extraordinarily tough; when they defeated him, they mined every last diamond. Behind, a creeper jumped out and exploded. Notch sprang away fast enough, but Herobrine was too slow and was blasted into a boiling lava pit. One day he will return to haunt Notch for eternity.

NOAH BENTLEY-SMALLEY (12)
West Sussex Alternative Provision College, Burgess Hill

ZOMBIE APOCALYPSE?

What the hell is going on? Where am I? Is this a hospital? I stand up to walk around and try to find somebody. Nobody's here. What's going on? It looks like this hospital is abandoned. I walk outside. It's strange. I can't hear anything. There's nobody out here, apart from dead bodies. I panic and wonder if this is real or is it a nightmare? Where is my family? Are they safe? I walk down the road and come across a man and his son. This is the last thing I see before it all goes black...

JAMIE DREW LUXFORD (14)
West Sussex Alternative Provision College, Burgess Hill

INVITATION TO THE BALL

Ink was splattered all over me this morning. Shortly after, I was put in an unlit, mysterious place then pushed through a thin rectangular opening. Bristles touched me before I thumped to the floor. Following the pain, two foul-smelling women grabbed me and light hit me. I couldn't bear the unpleasant smell, as they said together smiling, staring at me, 'You're invited to the prince's ball tomorrow night at 10pm.' High-pitched screaming hit my ears as I was scrunched into a ball and thrown to the ground. 'You're not invited,' they shouted, to a girl in rags; now crying.

ELLIE ADDISON (13)
Weydon School, Farnham

THE FAIRY GODMOTHER

She stubbed her half seared cigarette on the ashtray, covering it with burnt nicotine and tar. She had had only two clients to work with for that entire week, until she overheard speakers ringing into everyone's ear, implying the Fairy Godmother had to prepare for her next client. There was a very tricky dilemma however, she had to decide between two dresses, a blue and black one or a stunning blue tutu. She stood there for at least an hour with her chin in hand. She finally decided on the blue tutu. Off she went to her client... Cinderella.

AARON DAVIDS (13)
Weydon School, Farnham

NOT QUITE CINDERELLA

'Find whoever fits this slipper!' bellowed the prince.
Ministers searched towns and villages to find its owner. They had tried the old and infected, the young and zitty, but had no luck.
They came upon a large house and knocked. Out came three girls, two as ugly as pigs and one as pretty as flowers. Up stepped one of the uglies who had cut off one toe in hope, but to no avail. The second ugly had cut off all of her toes, it fitted!
The next day, she married the prince and Cinderella was left crying on the floor!

BEN ROOK (13)
Weydon School, Farnham

SPITEFUL SISTER

Alone, the innocent girl lay there. That monstrous being had heartlessly killed her, leaving her drenched in her own blood. Jealousy is a wicked emotion. The prince searched in pure desperation for his true devotion, clutching the glass slipper, remembering that magical night. He would venture through the downpour of the city to find her. By the edge of the silent stream lay the body. Approaching, he crippled over in horror, crawling towards her feet. He slipped on the slipper, it was a perfect fit. Realising, he lay there with his hand in hers and wept under the moonlit sky.

HOLLIE COCKRAM (12)
Weydon School, Farnham

127

CHUMMY'S TALE

There once was a time before man was fired, where Chummy was so innocent and sweet. That all changed when the curse was placed upon the lifeless doll. It became the devilish creature we now know today... Day after day, the doll sat on the shelves, our upcoming fate draws near. The story was never unmasked, but what we do know, a girl so innocent and sweet was the very first victim of this unfortunate killing spree. Chummy slew and slew until no man was alive. Each ear-piercing scream still echoes today around the world...

AIMEE DRAKE (13) & ISABELLE RICHARDS
Weydon School, Farnham

DINNER

The big bad wolf pounded on Grandma's door. *Knock! Knock!* It was so loud that all the local wildlife fled for cover. Grandma decisively opened the door... As quick as a flash, the Big Bad Wolf rushed into the house, knocking Grandma onto her weak, feeble back. Grandma panicked. She whipped out her AK47 and shot the wolf straight in the head with clear precision. She had been ready. The Big Bad Wolf fell to the ground and in his dying breath shouted, 'All I wanted was your nice, home-made chicken dinners... '

JOE EVERETT (15)
Willingdon Community School, Eastbourne

REVERSE GODZILLA

He was lonely. No one to talk to. His very breath sounded the gale of a damp winter's eve. He was scaly, serpentine in many aspects. He thought, not of love and compassion but of red. The red of crimson blood. His eyes gazed liked the sun's rays as he dragged his feet across the deserted, damp roads. No people, no love. His knife-sharp teeth could carve any meat into thin slices and his power could dominate the world. Again... He was still lonely. He had no place in human land. Did the humans kill him? Or was it himself?

JAMES BARTLETT (15)
Willingdon Community School, Eastbourne

BUTTONED

I'm Buttons, just a lonely servant boy who's really passionate about one thing, Cinderella. I think she's perfect; I'd love to be with her all the time. She also loves me, but not like I do. She says, 'Like a brother.' I know I don't stand a chance against Prince Charming, but I've hatched a plan. I've hired the world's top assassin to crash their wedding and kill Charming. Finally, I could be with the love of my life. Screaming and crying, she came running into my arms. I comforted her. And Charming? Well he's buttoned in his body bag.

BRYN SMITH (14)
Willingdon Community School, Eastbourne

ONCE UPON A TIME THE CLOCK STRUCK 12...

Cinderella, a wicked girl, was abandoned. So she was fostered by a wonderful family. Cinderella jumped at the chance of going to a ball. Her stepsisters were in rose petal dresses but she, however, was in the complete opposite. She caught a man's attention. The clock struck 12. She ran away, leaving her shoe. The man announced, 'Whoever this fits shall be my bride.' Cinderella saw this online the next day so ran to the town to try on the shoe. Of course it fitted, the wedding was planned and the man didn't know what he was in for...

LAUREN TAYLOR (14)
Willingdon Community School, Eastbourne

THE TYRANNY OF KING ARTHUR

'Keep up!' the king called to his son.
'Sorry Father,' the boy called out, sounding subdued as he kicked his horse into action.
'What's wrong?'
The young prince was surprised when he heard actual concern in his father's voice. 'Did you... did you really have to kill tho-... '
'Of course, they were peasants,' the king spat, brusquely cutting off the traitorous thoughts. 'Less important than the lowliest of creatures in Camelot. Their deaths mean nothing; you understand?'
'Yes... my king.' The heir to the kingdom stared at the ground - lingering images of charred corpses and bleeding children were forced away.

JACK PYE (15)
Willingdon Community School, Eastbourne

THE THREE LITTLE PIGS' NEW HOME

The pigs were kicked out of Mummy Pig's house. They needed a home. Upon walking through the woods they came to the outskirts of Slough. The first pig, Sanjay, suggested building a house from the leftover takeaway boxes they had along the way, but they didn't want the house to smell like fast food! The second oldest pig, Shaniqua, suggested building a house from Lego but Lego's extortionately overpriced! Eric, the oldest, purchased a one-bedroom apartment next to his mate Barry with cheap rent, Friendly neighbourhood, mediocre crime rate, run-of-the-mill living conditions... 'Good bargain!' said Eric.

MAX SALISBURY (15)
Willingdon Community School, Eastbourne

STRANGLED

It was her... the nefarious witch, Gothel, who took Rapunzel at birth. When the sun rose that morning, Rapunzel found a rattle from when she lay, wrapped in white, soundly in a cradle. Rapunzel noticed some engraved writing that had been scraped away. The princess looked closer and could see her name reflecting in the light. As she twizzled it in her hands the twinkle of light revealed the king's surname. It struck her. Rage roared, engulfing her body. To Gothel she plaited her way and wrapped her hair round her neck tightly.

MAISY MAYNARD-GRICE (14)
Willingdon Community School, Eastbourne

HUMPTY'S WARFARE

Humpty Dumpty was on the left side of Buckingham Palace, back on his favourite wall to sit on. However, this time his friends were with him. War had been declared against the army of humans, but Humpty's group of valiant eggs wouldn't give up without a fight. They would not fall off the wall. Suddenly, Humpty unleashed his special weapon. His latest fall off the wall had given him a permanent scar. A crack. Suddenly he realised his mistake. A cooked grenade came out of his crack. The army of eggs was now a feast of omelettes! Silly Humpty Dumpty.

KYLE VIJAY VAGHELA (14)
Wilson's School, Wallington

THE DUMPING

He sat there, looking over the city and he slowly gazed at the sun, losing himself in the mesmerising colours. True beauty, the last he saw. He was shoved off the ledge and fell down, wind running through his hair as he plummeted to his inevitable death. He crashed down to the pavement. Blood leaked out of his gaping mouth and blood trickled from his head, his cracked head almost like an egg. People gathered around him. Paramedics took him away. Policemen on horses followed them. They imported the body to Humpty and he dumped the body in a river.

JORDAN DOBBS (14)
Wilson's School, Wallington

WHAT'S THAT UNDER YOUR BED?

Silence... the room seemed to close in on them. To the left, a fake window, the right, a sealed door with Satanic carvings. There was a dim brazier in the middle with 8 beds circling it, of which 4 were empty. The silence was deafening. The children's eyes filled with fear. They had to keep the fire burning they had to keep it alive, or it would crawl among the darkness and strike with its might. They remembered a bit of its rhyme: 'What's under your bed? Spitting, snarling with spite... Keep the fire burning little children, or you'll die...
'

MINH-NHAT NGUYEN (14)
Wilson's School, Wallington

THE DECISION

I lie close to the rooftop's edge, its positioning perfect to execute my fiendish plan. The icy wind which hits me, sends shivers down my spine and feels like a knife on my neck. I know I can end my suffering tonight with one pull of the trigger. The pain she caused me was unbearable, but now I can solve my problem. For some reason I cannot bear to do it. I will not become a murderer, so I now know what I have to do. I glimpse the cartridge shooting towards me and the pain ceases.

DANIEL ALLCHIN (14)
Wilson's School, Wallington

133

Arthur Pengingerbread

Ping! I heard the oven, ready. I was ready. Yes, I was ready. I am Arthur, Arthur the gingerbread man. I'd planned that as soon as I was out, I would run away. As soon as the baker took me out of the oven, I headed for the exit. A few days went past and this was the life! Suddenly, I heard a noise. I looked and it was a fox. I backed up and stumbled across a big rock with a sword in it. I pulled out Excalibur and swung it at the fox and cut him open.

Aakas Ravikumaran (14)
Wilson's School, Wallington

The Anonymous Predator

My friend and I were at the pub down my road after another day at work. The sky was a shade of misty grey, with a sharp, powerful breeze. My friend left to find his wallet, but his departure was followed by an ear-splitting noise. Blood on the floor, and an object like a bodily organ lay beside it. A shiver went down my spine, like a bucket of ice had been poured down my neck. My stomach felt like spiders were crawling over it. On the wall, read: 'Man was made for survival, but survival was not made for Man'.

Amaan Hassan (14)
Wilson's School, Wallington

ALONE IN THE FOREST

I stared through the eternal darkness. Pitch-black. Sounds of footsteps crept behind my back. I froze. Tentatively, I twisted my head, my heart racing with fear. Suddenly, within the depths of the dark, a face appeared. Its rotten teeth were as green as slime. Its mouth widened, its grin as though Christmas had come early. In the corner of my eye, I saw droplets of crimson dripping slowly. It was eating something, shiny... flesh.
I carefully tiptoed, trying not to alert the monster. However, its eyes were closely fixed on my body. I was next...

JEFFREY KAN (14)
Wilson's School, Wallington

THE SKY WAS BLACK

The sky was black, the smell of death wasting through the blocks towering the deserted city. No voice could be heard, but in the shadows stood a dark man on a dark mission. Eyes tied to every moving object, like an eagle hunting for prey. He watched a man walking into a post office. He ran. He ran fast. Hesitantly, he ran faster. Oblivious to the consequences, he crept into the post office, a lion ready to pounce. Lifting the gun slowly, he pulled the trigger, remembering he had no choice. Ready, he took a deep breath. It was done.

RAHEEM BUTT (14)
Wilson's School, Wallington

135

The Crazed Rapunzel

She sits silently, staring blankly into the wall, into the number 13.
She looks at her arm, still seeing the number 13 carved into her skin.
Wherever she looks in her horrid cell, she sees it. She hears the
incessant dripping drops of water, 13 every minute. She creeps like
a bug to the other side of the chamber, picking up a sharp stone and
filling in the final space on the wall. She hears the church bells ring
13 times for the 13,000th time. She slings her hair out the window
and follows it, falling to her death.

LINUS BOSELIUS (14)
Wilson's School, Wallington

The Seed

Jack rummaged through his pockets, trying to find his only
possession - the seed. Sweat poured down Jack's muddy face as
he finally found it. He knew that the Grimm brothers hid all their fairy
tales in the seed, never to be opened. Then they appeared. 'We want
that back!' the Grimms cried, synchronised in speech. 'The moment
you open the seed, you'll release all hell!'
'You put me here!' Jack screamed, digging his long, sharp nails into
the seed. The seed let out a raucous cry, dropping Jack to his knees.
Then the world he knew, vanished before his eyes.

BYRON SUTHERLAND
Wilson's School, Wallington

Worlds Colliding

Ariel basked in the golden sunlight. Swimming under coral and through schools of fish. Life was good. Flounder swam beside her, commenting about this and that. Ariel glared up at a human's ship. A big metal beast that Eric had told her about. This one was different. It was tipped over and there was a dark substance flowing out. Ariel moved closer. The darkness snaked towards her. Ariel reached out. The darkness leapt. It consumed her, covering her whole body and stealing her breath. As her vision began to fade, she looked up to the ship and the letters BP.

Ieuan Grainger (13)
Wilson's School, Wallington

Ashes To Ashes

Life and death. Love and hatred. Passion and madness. Jealousy and guilt. Every day I live through the latter in each of those sentences. Crossing from grave to grave, I am not really sure what I am doing with my life. Am I the gatekeeper to Heaven... or Hell? Do I bring grief and pain or pride and joy? I have a knife in my hand and wear the same slacks every day. I see dead bodies burning. Floods of tears pour to the ground. Ashes to ashes, dust to dust, I am a murderer, I have nobody to trust.

Janaken Prabhakaran (13)
Wilson's School, Wallington

BAMBI'S DAY

The forests of Saxony were filled with the most incredible of creatures. Among them lived Bambi and her fawn. Day after day, Bambi nurtured her young, collecting food and leaves for shelter. One day when Bambi returned, her fawn had vanished. Wind rustled through the trees, covering the ground in leaves, but a trail of footprints remained. Bambi ambled into the swamp of the deep, dark woods. Bambi struggled towards the cave. A light sat above a witch's pot. Behind her she heard the howl of a wolf approaching and turned and saw a trotter protruding out of its neck.

MORGAN ANTHONY (14)
Wilson's School, Wallington

THE CANNIBAL

The gingerbread cannibal sprang into the forest with the hearts of the witches attached to its gingery body like chocolate buttons, its appearance as gruesome as its creator's. Nearby, the innocent Little Red was trudging along carrying her basket of meringues destined for her grandmother. It smelt the enticing scent of the other and at that point, they came face-to-face, a girl and an abomination. It ripped the other's body to shreds and swallowed the gory flesh whole. Little Red had enjoyed her meal. 'What a strong ginger!' There was more than one cannibal roaming this forest.

THARSHAN KUHENDIRAN (13)
Wilson's School, Wallington

THINK OF THE EMPLOYEES! IT'S NOT THEIR FAULT

Oh dear. Another pesky employee has died. That means more paperwork for me. That 'spy' fellow really needs to think about the workers of this criminal syndicate hell bent on world domination. I can hear him now, getting closer. I'm almost done. Just going to cash in my life insurance. All of the paperwork's in order. Oh he's here now. 'Hey you! wait a second. I'm just going to finish this and go.' 'Too slow, the name's Bond by the way.' He's going to shoot me. This Bond fellow really is cocky. I'm sure we'll find a way to kill...

KIERAN REHAL (14)
Wilson's School, Wallington

THE DAY OF A LONG DOWNFALL OF GOLDEN HAIR

He streamed along in the darkness. On horseback he was 13 feet tall with a long billowing cloak streaming behind him. A crown gleamed beneath his black hood as he climbed to the makeshift tree house 60 feet up a giant Sacoya. He took out the stand and set it up. He took a single dart out of his bag and placed it on the track of his crossbow. His headshot was waiting for him. And he shot. The dart rifled towards the tower window and hit a target, but not the right one. His long-haired love had fallen.

VOU-FRI SETT (14)
Wilson's School, Wallington

DON'T TRUST ANYONE

Jack and Jill were good friends. Jill's boyfriend, Josh, was very handsome and Jill really liked him, but she didn't know that Jack liked her very much. Josh and Jill were very happy together, but this made Jack very angry, 'Grrr!'
One day, Jack invited Josh to go and collect some water from the well. Josh agreed and so they went up the hill to fetch a pail of water. They got to the top and Jack let Josh get the water. Jack then pulled a knife out of his pocket and stabbed Josh four times in the skull. Dead.

JOSH EVES (14)
Wilson's School, Wallington

THE BEANSTALK'S RESURRECTION

Jack takes the axe his mother used. There was a slimy green substance. Jack ran in horror back outside. There lay the evil transformation of the beanstalk. Spikes pierced out of its body and a head grew almost immediately with menacing teeth and the jaw of a crocodile. Solid, rapid wheels emerged from its body and rotated like a drill. The beanstalk flattened over Jack's mum like stepping on a grape, and it unleashed itself through the house. It demolished the house and wrapped itself around the small cottage until it reached the top, with Jack's body in its mouth.

ANOJAN KIRITHARAN (14)
Wilson's School, Wallington

YOUNG WRITERS INFORMATION

We hope you have enjoyed reading this book – and that you will continue to in the coming years.

If you're a young writer who enjoys reading and creative writing, or the parent of an enthusiastic poet or story writer, do visit our website www.youngwriters.co.uk. Here you will find free competitions, workshops and games, as well as recommended reads, a poetry glossary and our blog.

If you would like to order further copies of this book, or any of our other titles give us a call or visit **www.youngwriters.co.uk**.

Young Writers
Remus House
Coltsfoot Drive
Peterborough
PE2 9BF

(01733) 890066 / 898110
info@youngwriters.co.uk